CONTENTS

To papa: the most creative, insightful, hilarious, caring, and, after all, genius father a person could have. Story after story, game after game, joke after joke, your ideas spark mine. I love you.

CHAPTER ONE

The Crack in the Ceiling

THE CRACK IN THE ceiling must have been staring at me for a while.

My sweaty fingers felt heavy on my face. They burned as they touched my heating forehead, and with all my might I pulled my hand off. I felt so tired, so weak. It was strange, because I've always been very healthy.

I turned my eyes to the carpet, something new to look at. Strangely, the horse weave on the rug seemed to speak to me.

I saw the pile of paper on my desk, I saw the pen, and I saw the horse on the blue rug. The horse moved, and suddenly, I was moving on it. The crack opened, creating an oasis of sand to come pouring in. Cactuses sprouted in an instant. My pale, green painted walls became a bright yellow, and instead of the cool air that should have been blowing on me from my fan, I felt a dry wind wisp across the room.

Δ Δ Δ

Lee Cot, western cowboy, sped on his horse through the barren desert. His entire life was behind him. He was moving toward danger: he could smell it.

But in front of him was a group of horses, and the leader of the pack seemed to be flat, like a rug with a blue background. This was not the desert he should have been in. Not what it had appeared to be before this day.

He shook his head, and galloped forward. Suddenly, the sky changed from a light shade of green to a glistening blue with a strong, hot sun. Now Cot wasn't sure whether he was imagining things or not.

But he needed to focus on the Mountain of Life. This life changing, life telling, life prophetic Mountain was the whole point of this journey. You see, Cot lived in a very unusual though typical, fantasized world: there was the good, and the evil. Yes, it was classic for a "magic" world. But this era of magic was a bit different from all the others.

Every decade, or so the people thought, a new chapter of life was summoned to begin. And so every ten years, some sort of punctuation mark was to be placed on top of the Mountain of Life to determine the future of the upcoming years. Either one person from the Good Side or the Bad Side of the world was to have the honor of placing a mark.

But it wasn't such an honor anymore. This last decade had been so anarchic! So chaotic, so disordered, so, so unusually, surprisingly… well, strange! Precisely ten years ago, an exclamation mark had been placed onto the Mountain and had led the following years into craze. Everyone wanted revolution, despite the fact that they didn't even know what for. Everyone wanted to party for some unknown reason. Everyone wanted everything and everything wanted everyone! Yes, it was in some ways uproarious but in other ways plain mad.

Everyone somewhat craved these strange events except for four theoretical people. Two were from the Good Side, and two from the Bad. These people consisted of King G. Ood and Lee Cot from the Good Side, and Villain B. Ad and Sir E. Vil from the more Evil Side.

Ugh. What a mix of people. The one, one and only matter they agreed upon was that they never, ever would let an exclamation mark be put onto the sacred Mountain again.

There was a rather big problem, however. Because although they all agreed they did not want any upcoming years to be like the last ten, they wanted completely different futures.

Villain B. Ad, the King of the Bad Side, was very troubled with his life at this point in time, or so Lee Cot had heard. He was so fed up with life, with the world, with the people, and with the constant bothersome events that were occurring that he wanted everything, and that goes for everyone, to end. And so his solution was to send Sir. E. Vil with a giant period onto the Mountain of Life.

Now as every person knows, periods are a representation of endings grammatically, metaphorically, and literally. But the only time that a period had been placed onto the Mountain of Life was years ago, hundreds of years ago, and that had created the Black Years. During the Black Years, everyone had gone on in despair. And even though life hadn't really ended, all the joys and pleasures of it had. People sulked constantly, and another happy moment didn't exist until 50 years later, when King G. Ood was born.

He had rescued the citizens of the Magic World from the Black Years. And it wasn't until now that someone had wanted the Dark Ages to repeat.

It wasn't necessarily that Villain B. Ad wanted the Black Years to happen again. In fact, he didn't take any thought to it. The selfish king was so fed up, and to him, the whole world deserved to be sewn up and thrown away.

Meanwhile, on the other side of the planet, King G. Ood and Lee Cot were heavily discussing political matters. Yes, the future was a very political matter.

They eagerly agreed that a question mark on the Mountain of Life would be the best way to go. That was the only mark that wouldn't hurt the world but that would also give it great advantages. With the question mark, life would be one, long sentence of unanswered questions and new possibilities. Life would not be an endpoint or a finish line; it would only be the new step to continuing, to understanding.

Lee Cot had no doubt that the King and him were right. That was why he was galloping at high speed in a sandy dessert under a blazing sun: because he knew. And not only did he know, he was ready to take action.

CHAPTER TWO

Mr. Bombompsky

MR. BOMBOMPSKY ALWAYS WORE purple satin Indian
slippers to not match (or rather in contrast) with his black suit coat
with yellow hexagonal shaped buttons. He had three pairs of black
socks and three pairs of brown socks, which he mixed to make six pairs
of brown/black socks. He liked his socks a little big for room to stretch
his toes.

"Mr. Bompomsky, your eel-avocado roll is here."

Mr. Bombompsky blinked. He was at Yamato, the Japanese restaurant
he dined at every Tuesday.

"Thank you, Saki Motto." Saki Motto was Mr. Bombompsky's
favorite waiter, and he requested him as his server each time he went to
the restaurant.

He sat at the table and bit into the eel. The fish was brought to the
restaurant every Monday night, and Mr. Bombompsky always came on
Tuesday for the fresh fish lunch special.

As he tapped his #3 pencil on the table, he remembered his days as a (semi) famous Ukrainian drummer. He still loved to make a beat out of anything.

Mr. Bombompsky came to Yamato every Tuesday because Tuesday was his thinking day. And of course, eating eel-avocado rolls made his novels even better. Eating eel-avocado rolls increased his imagination.

Mr. Bombompsky looked down at his purple satin slippers, wondering where to take his characters; what to do with his book. Should Lee Cot go forward in his journey, or should the story go back and focus on Emil, who through his illness was writing about Cot? As he contemplated this, he knew he needed to make his book a quadruple Nobel Prize winner.

He ate another roll. He ate more and more eel, until his imagination overpowered him.

Δ Δ Δ

Later that night, Mr. Bombompsky started packing for the book conference he planned to attend in Marseille. His flight was on Thursday, and as today was Tuesday, he did not have much time. He sat on the bed, hopeless; he was too busy thinking about his book to pack.

"Why not?" he said to himself.

Even though he knew no one else was there, he looked sheepishly around the room to check if anybody was watching. He knew he had to pack, but couldn't bring himself to do it. His desk was four feet away from the bed, and his notepad with his lucky #3 pencil was on it. He slowly walked to the desk, sat down, and began.

CHAPTER THREE

My Grandma the Wrestler

FAR OFF IN THE distance, Cot saw a blurry outline of a man—a

stranger on a big, big horse. The man was wearing a tall, black hat and some sort of cape was fluttering in the wind against his back.

Something went off in Cot's mind. An image of a man on a horse, in a similar desert to the one he was in now. He was climbing up a mountain, pushing up a wheelbarrow with something very heavy in it. He was approaching the very top of the mountain, and gold light seemed to be shining on a platform close to the man. But before the man could go down to see what was inside, another man, the stranger with a tall, black top hat and a cape fluttering in the wind, took out a gun.

Smoke was everywhere. Someone had been shot.

Lee Cot put his hands on his head. What was going on?

Then he faintly remembered something King G. Ood had told him before he left on his mission. "You and I are somewhat telekinetic, somehow clairvoyant. And that unique ability will come in handy someday. Maybe even while you're gone. I just want you to remember,

Cot, that you may visualize, or should I say see some strange pictures, some strange images in your mind. Don't think you're hallucinating. Because it may be that someone is sending you a messa-" That was all he remembered.

He squinted, trying to see the man in the distance more clearly. The moon was not very full tonight, and did not give off much light. Cot took in a heavy breath, got off his horse, retrieved some food from his pack, fed his horse, fed himself, and set up camp. They both laid down, and while watching the magnificent sky full of glowing stars, fell into a deep, restful sleep.

Δ Δ Δ

I looked up from my writing. I could hear my grandma walking up the stairs to my room. It sounded like thunder: either she had grown, or she was bringing up something that weighed a ton.

I sniffled. Even though I couldn't smell very well because my nose was so stuffed up, I sniffed the aroma of Grandma Gertrude's chicken soup. Ugh. I quickly hid my writing under my mattress. Grandma usually wouldn't let me do anything but sleep or just lay in bed when I was sick.

"Emil, are you awake?" She said in her loud voice, while knocking.

"Yes," I sighed.

She came in through the door, but had kind of a hard time getting in. I hadn't wanted anyone to disturb me while I was writing so I had piled up all my toys, most of my books, my dresser, and my green bean bag chair against the door.

But my grandma was as strong as ever. She also had a very unique style and personality, and not in a way one could say was good or bad. She spent half of each day at the gym, so she was very muscular and had a very sturdy body, unlike me, but it looked slightly peculiar because she had wrinkles all over. Plus, while she "loved to work out," she always made sure she was dressed over appropriately for the occasion, in my opinion. Once, my parents had to attend a special work meeting, so I had to go to the gym with her. Her gym outfit that day was a long linen skirt, no shorts under, which apparently she wore on her first date with my grandpa. It had velvet flowers all over it. She also wore a beaded tank top and long, purple dangly earrings that matched her purple painted toenails. I shuddered at the thought. As one could probably imagine, it looked so strange with her big body and her wrinkly face, which was aimed to be covered up with mascara but in reality had turned out to cause her face to turn a bright pink, permanently, which she covered up with a mask, but of course she chose a clear mask, which makes no sense whatsoever, 'cause you could see her wrinkles. What a character. She had so many sides to her. At this point, I don't know if she's a fat old lady, a dinosaur, or just my grandma from Denmark.

Eventually finding her way through the maze of my attempt at a barrier, she came into my room holding a tray with a big bowl of her chicken soup, some crackers, and a tall mug of hot tea.

"Thank you... Grandma," I managed to say.

I'm pretty sure that when she was little, she got no appreciation whatsoever, so now, even if it's completely obvious that a person is faking their gratitude, she will accept any little compliment. She smiled real big at me.

"Oh, it's nothing. Anything for my favorite little grandson!" She came over to me and squeezed my cheeks incredibly hard.

"Now, I'm going downstairs to start your dinner. Remember to dip the crackers in the soup, honey."

"Yes."

The second she left the room, I went into the bathroom, poured half of the soup in the toilet, flushed it, poured most of the tea in the sink and proceeded to wash it out. I put the tray outside of my room, closed the door, and pushed back my beanbag and dresser against it. I really, just, don't like overly kind people. I guess I should feel bad about it... but I don't.

I took out my notebook.

CHAPTER FOUR

Cooking the Character

MR. BOMBOMPSKY SMILED. HE was very satisfied with what he had written.

He turned to the page with his notes on Emil's grandmother. He started to think more about her. She was the hardest character to write for him because he had never known either of his own grandmothers. He began to remember his old friend, Vince Tuckler, and the many afternoons they had spent together at his house. Vince's grandma would always be patiently standing at the door, waiting for them to hop off the bus that brought them home from school. She always waited for them with a volcano of steaming chocolate chip cookies piled high and oozing molten chocolate from hidden crevices. She watched the boys when Vince's parents were at work.

Mr. Bombompsky never had someone waiting for him at home, so he admired Vince's grandmother a great deal. As a child, his parents were always at work as well, but his mother's parents had passed away, and his father's parents were rather aggressive and didn't get along with the family. Even though Mrs. Tuckler's cookies were often burnt, Mr. Bombompsky had found it comforting to be around her. Emil's grandma was based on Vince's. The one thing, however, that wasn't similar was obsession. His description of Emil's grandma was, well, nice. Too nice! Mr. B didn't know how to explain it. Overall, he was just trying to capture the life of a ten-year-old boy. He hoped Emil was the reality of a kid: after all, childhood was what he was trying to explore in his writing.

Mr. Bombompsky leaned his head back in his chair and stretched his arms out, the kind of stretch an author does after sitting at his desk writing for a long, long time.

He got up and went to his kitchen. Just three weeks ago, Mr. Bombompsky's kitchen had been remodeled. Along with all his other passions, he thought it was vital to have an inviting cooking space, especially for a writer like himself. The kitchen was only another room of delectable possibilities.

Mr. Bombompsky spent hours in his kitchen, cooking up delicious meals, and, every time he was working on a book, he tried to cook the characters as well. He tried to create the characters through cooking by adding spices, choosing what country the food was originally from, whether it was fresh food or canned food; if the character was a vegetarian, a vegan; if they were stranded on an island, what would they eat, etc.

That night, for dinner, he decided he would have a three-course meal based on Lee Cot. He opened his laptop and researched ethnic food of… of the desert?

He couldn't quite find the answer to that, so he decided the meal would have a kind of classical Tex-Mex spicy-ish flavor.

But he wanted to add more to Lee Cot. He felt spices from Morocco, nuts, chili with cheese, pickles (of course), prosciutto, and adventurous white wine. Lee Cot would not be shy to new things: he would have a sturdy mind and would know exactly what he liked.

"That's it," Mr. Bombompsky said to himself. "That's it."

There would be a fried sea bass covered in mushrooms, spicy cashews, almonds, and raisins with fresh squeezed lemon. With that would come an heirloom tomato salad, topped with sea salt, pepper, oil, and feta cheese. It would also come with lightly toasted pita covered in hummus. All of that, however, was the éntre. The first course, an appetizer, would be two kinds of bread. One, baked with melted brie cheese and prosciutto, and the second one, a French baguette—simple but delicious, dipped in a homemade olive oil served with a platter of olives. For dessert, well, that would come to him after he made the first two courses. Not exactly your typical western cowboy, but hey! This was Lee Cot, Mr. Bombompsky's cooked up creation.

Mr. Bombompsky decided to invite over a few of his friends, a tradition for character meals. He took out his phone and dialed Saki Motto, who blissfully accepted.

Then Mr. Bombompsky called his good friend from the Writers Weekly Newspaper (WWN), Liza Dempsey. She could make it as well.

"Hello, Mr. Cordele. It's Mr. Bombompsky."

"Hi, Mr. B! How goes it?"

"Well, I'm having a character meal tonight, and Liza and my good friend Saki Motto will be there." He didn't even have to extend an invitation.

"I'll be right over. I'd be a fool to miss one of these meals!"

Now, Mr. Bombompsky just had to start cooking.

CHAPTER FIVE

Ida Cremchanskivich

IDA CREMCHANSKIVICH'S STOMACH RUMBLED. She was so deep in thought about her book that she had forgotten to eat, and at this point wasn't even sure where she was. She was supposed to be eating dinner on the airplane, but her Lufthansa flight had been delayed. As she looked around, she remembered. Her stomach rumbled again.

She sat on the metal chairs (with little cushioning) of the airport while looking at her watch, saying over and over again to herself, "Why is my plane so late?" all the while trying to read her book. It was 03h13 Italy time and 22h13 New York time, where she lived. She now was stuck in the Favignana airport in Sicily waiting for a airplane to fly back to Germany where she would transfer planes to go back home. The flight had been delayed from a 01h30 flight to a 03h00 one. Ida assumed it was never going to come.

She looked around the airport. She saw all these tired people, waiting; looking at their watches, playing games they didn't even like but just needing to do something to pass the endless time. There were also all the restaurants and shops, most of them closed. She imagined herself sitting on a Central Park bench, eating a hotdog with sauerkraut and mustard from her favorite pushcart peddler, Benny.

Ah. She smiled at the wonderful thought.

She quickly looked back at her book. If it weren't for the fact that she was enormously in need of some nourishment (in the form of FOOD), her eyes would be glued to the page.

Ida had read so many interesting books throughout her life. And many of them she had loved so much that she read them each in one day. But at times, she felt like she had never read them just because she had read them too fast.

Ida was trying to savor this story. She was at the best part: Mr. Bombompsky, an author who was in the process of writing a book, was having a "character meal" to describe the top creation of his new book: the character was Lee Cot, a western cowboy. She was saving this part to read on the plane so the ride wouldn't be such a bore.

She held out her hands dreamily like she was eating a hotdog, and took a bite. She made a chewing motion with her jaw and smiled at the wonderful taste. She took an imaginary napkin from her pocket and wiped her mouth. Ah.

She blinked and noticed a women sitting next to her staring. Ida smiled a fake smile, as she just remembered what she was doing. She shook her head and made a silent laugh.

Ida Cremchanskivich yawned and lay down on her book. She tried to fall asleep but couldn't. Her mind drifted off, dreaming about Lee Cot. Would he get that question mark up to the top of the Mountain of Life? She couldn't wait to find out.

"Ladies and gentleman of Terminal 4, flying on Lufthansa, with the destination of Berlin Tegel, we are now boarding. First class passengers, please come to the gate," came a thick Italian voice from the loud speaker.

Ida shot up like bullet, rubbed her eyes, then quickly put her glasses back on. She straightened her back, picked up her bags (a magenta and maroon rolling duffel and a purse), and was ready to go.

By the time they called the economy class passengers, Ida was already standing at the gate, ready (as ready as one can be) to take off. First in the line, she gave the ticket agent her boarding pass and finally got on the plane.

Ida tried to get comfortable in the not so comfortable plane seats. She took out her iPod and listened to her absolute favorite song, a piano piece by Aldo Ciccolini, and then proceeded to listen to some Glen

Gould. As she listened and embraced the notes of the piano in the song, she found herself saying in her head, "I am so lucky to be sitting at the window." She looked toward the plump old lady two spots over on the aisle. Ida watched her try to squeeze her young son into the seat between them. The boy cringed with frustration.

Ida took out her book.

CHAPTER SIX

A Night of Music

WITH THE FIRST TWO courses leaving an excellent impression,

they started the "desert" dessert of a cactus themed coconut cream pie. The meal had been very satisfactory, and everything had gone as planned. Mr. Cordele had brought his wife, and she and Liza were happily chatting. Mr. Bombompsky, Mr. Cordele, and Saki Motto were having a three-way conversation about the major declines of the stock market. Mr. Bombompsky argued it was another depression, but Mr. Cordele had faith in the United States, while Saki Motto didn't know the half of it but was just listening in.

As they finished eating and the conversations dialed down a bit, Mr. Bombompsky decided it was time for music.

"Excuse me for a moment," he said to his guests, who were now rubbing their stomachs happily and sipping the fruity dessert wine—a sugar laden, spicy grape Gewürztraminer—that Liza had brought.

Mr. Bombompsky went to the bookcase. He pressed a button, and behind the wall appeared a music room with his Lithuanian drum set in the center. Along the walls were records, pictures of famous musicians, and instruments hung up. Mr. Bombompsky had an exceptional house. It was a three-story brownstone; he lived on two floors and rented out the other. When it came to real estate, Mr. Bombompsky was an expert. He had come into the market at a very good time, and he took advantage of it. He had had a lot of money in his savings account, so he went ahead and bought three brownstones in Brooklyn: one as his own home, and two other four story ones as rental properties. He made good money through these homes, which also allowed him to be a writer. He knew that if he didn't make good money through his books, he would always have a back up. But Mr. Bombompsky had done very well in both careers. Because of this, he was able to afford many things of quality, and he spent his money well.

Everyone gasped. His music room was very new.

"Mr. Bombompsky, I didn't know you were a famous musician!" Saki Motto exclaimed.

Mr. Bombompsky raised his eyebrows up and down, and smiled. "Okay, everybody. Come on, nothing's wrong with splurging! Now let me just take the plates in and we're going to turn this house into a music hall!"

All his guests, as if on cue, said, "Can we help?"

Mr. Bombompsky shrugged, in a way that said you shouldn't because you're a guest but why not? They all brought in the dishes.

"Everyone, welcome to the Whirl Pool of Sound! I thought it was an interesting name," he laughed.

"What about your neighbors?" asked Mr. Cordele, who was very cautious about interruption.

"What about them? I'm sure they'll love to hear some music. Something else to do other than sit at their couches all day, listening to those people on CNN."

Together the guests went inside the room, and each chose an instrument. Mr. Bombompsky sat on the leather stool drumming on his set: a Tama with an exotic lacquer finish. It was his prized possession. Mr. Cordele lightly hit a tambourine, his wife shook the shakers, Saki Motto played a Japanese song on the harmonica, and Liza strummed a classy western tune on her guitar.

The house was filled with sound for hours. Sometimes, the ensemble sounded really quite good, but other times, well, you could just say they were experimenting. But all the guests had a very, very pleasurable time.

By 11:00 at night, they were still playing. Mr. Bombompsky brought out a platter of chocolate chip cookies. Liza brought took out a log of homemade nougat and Mr. and Mrs. Cordele poured dessert wine for everyone, while Saki Motto gave everyone a bowl of Japanese green-tea ice cream. They ate all the desserts with much satisfaction, and even though crumbs got everywhere, Mr. Bombompsky was having so much fun that he didn't care.

Δ Δ Δ

"Would you like anything to drink?"

"Huh?" Ida looked up to see a stewardess holding a tray of drinks. "Oh. Yes. May I have a hot water?"

"Lemon?"

"Please," she replied.

As Ida slowly sipped her hot water with the pulp of the squeezed lemon, she started thinking about how nice it would be when she got home; home to her piano, home to her apartment, home to Benny the pushcart peddler with fresh hot-dogs waiting for her everyday.

But then she remembered that her connecting flight had been delayed. That meant that she would miss the flight from Berlin to New York. Oy, she muttered to herself. She put her hands on her face and shook her head.

She might have to stay overnight in Berlin. But that would cost a lot of money, and Ida was saving her money to purchase a grand, grander than grand piano.

Ida recalled she had a friend who lived in Berlin. She had known this woman since she was very little. They were both raised in Russia, but then Ida emigrated to New York, and her friend married a German man and also moved away.

Ida wasn't that fond of her old friend anymore, but if she could stay the night at her house, she would save about 120 Euros; 70 for a hotel, 20 for a cab ride, and 30 for food. She could manage one night with her old friend.

Though maybe she wouldn't need to. Maybe her flight home would not be delayed. Maybe she could spare a lucky penny. If she wasn't lucky, however, she would have no way of finding her friend. She hadn't contacted her in years; all she could remember was that her name was Antje Schröder, and she was married to someone by the name of Erich Schröder, and that they had two kids and, no doubt, still lived in Berlin.

Ida would figure that out later. The only thing that excited her was that she would be able to go to Café Au Lait. When Ida was younger, she traveled to Berlin many times, because she had entered a piano competition that had taken place in there. She had discovered the Café on the morning of the contest. The elderberry had soothed her nervousness. She had always dreamed of going back.

For some reason, Ida loved the Café's elderberry tea—a luxurious blend of berries magically formed into a luscious drink. She had never heard of it before she tried it there, but the minute she tasted the tea, she knew it was made for her. If it weren't for the fact that she had many other things to do, she would come to Berlin just to get a sip of that tea. It was because of that discovery that she began her love of tea-drinking. She had begun to explore all the American tea brands, but never found any of them as wonderful as the elderberry tea. IKEA made an Elderflower juice that came in a box, but it tasted fake to her. The only American brand that she sort of liked was Tazo Tea. She liked this brand not really because of the taste, which wasn't that special, but because on each of the tea bags, there was an interesting quote.

In fact, she just remembered why she had asked for hot water. Since one can't bring liquids on the plane, Ida had brought a numerous amount of Tazo Tea packets. She took one out from her handbag and read the message: *Beatles and bugs and ants will keep living, but where will you go when the sun starts dimming?* She ripped it open, plopped in her cup, and stirred. She sipped her tea, finally with a little real satisfaction.

Ida wished she could listen to the music Mr. Bombompsky and his friends had made. She wanted something new from her piano.

She had gone to Italy for a vacation because she thought she needed a break.

But every second of every minute of almost every hour, she dreamt of being back in her apartment, playing the piano. Sometimes she would start moving her fingers around, trying to play. Each time, she forgot where she was. And her pieces were constantly echoing through her mind.

Sometimes she held her hands to her head and tried to figure out why she was so in love with this instrument. The one thing that had helped her through these moments was composing her own piano pieces. On her trip, she had written three pages of music without even getting to play them. Maybe even a fourth page, actually. Nothing she could do would get the music out of her mind. So the music stayed like a nonstop, repeating loop in her head, and she heard it constantly. When she went on a tour of the ancient temples in Rome, everyone could hear her humming. It was as if her humming made the temples come alive, and everyone around her could feel the energy of the ancients surrounding them.

Everyone enjoyed it, though. The people accompanying her on the tour had asked if she was a professional musician. She didn't know what to say to that, so just smiled and said, "I am the living female Mozart." That was who she hoped she was.

Ida thought her response would make people laugh, and send them away saying she was a crazy old woman, but it did the opposite. People became fascinated with her. They watched her, yet she wasn't aware of the curiosity they had with her music. Ida wasn't trying to impress people. She just felt a sudden urge of happiness which she expressed through her humming and composition. And people seemed to love it.

She sipped her passion Tazo Tea.

"Excuse me?" Ida heard someone say. She turned and looked to see the young boy with strawberry colored hair next to her. He was wearing a red t-shirt and cargo shorts with lots of pockets.

"What's your name?" he asked in a British accent, a sound that Ida always had loved to hear.

"Willy, please," his mother said, looking sheepishly at Ida.

"Oh, its okay. My name is Ida. Is yours Willy?" she said.

Ida never understood why some parents were so embarrassed when their child simply asked a stranger a question. Her parents had done the same thing, and she always wondered why.

"Yup! And this is my mum. I'm seven! She's older, I think! Why are you going to Germany?" Willy asked, grinning.

"I live in New York, and I'm supposed to transfer planes once we get to Berlin. What about you?"

"I'm just on a vacation. I live in Liverpool, England. We're going to visit my mum's sister and my cousins."

"Oh!" Ida replied, then looked back to her book.

Mr. Bombompsk-

"Can you tell me a story? I desperately want to fall asleep, and I can't without a jolly good story. It's so important; it's Willy tradition! Please?" Willy's voice came out.

Ida looked up and followed Willy's gaze to his mom. Willy's mom (Ida decided to call her Mrs. Willy) tried to speak once again, but she sounded like a mute, speaking though saying nothing, motioning with huge gestures.

"My mum's voice is all gone from yelling at me, so she can't tell me one," he finished, almost bursting out with laughter.

Ida looked at Willy, then to his mom. By this point, Mrs. Willy was ignoring her son's questions and working on a book of "Extra-Easy" Sudoku.

"There once was a land with no rain. It was bare, as dry as a skeleton bone. The orchards had dried up; the crispy, delectable apples had turned rotten and sour. Flocks and flocks of sheep, cattle, and even the birds had no energy to do anything. Especially the people. One hot, sunny, dry, scorching night, under the moon, along the dried river bend came a young woman with flowing golden blond curly hair. Seeing this curious woman, the town gathered around her. The woman started to sing, her voice making the most beautiful ranges of sound. The sad music awakened their eyes, and they started to cry. They cried through the entire night, and as the song started to become softer, as if to soothe the citizens eyes, the rivers filled, the empty bottles in everyone's straw homes filled with cool, blue, clear liquid, and golden apples burst from the trees. Finally, the city was reborn once again: with water, life, and happiness."

Ida looked at Willy. He was lying on his mom; sleeping, muttering, "water, finally", and he had the most calm, delightful look on his face Ida had ever seen.

"The end," she whispered.

With Willy sleeping, she opened the book.

CHAPTER SEVEN

The Author Behind the Author

MR. BOMBOMPSKY STRETCHED HIS arms and rubbed his eyes. The afternoon light was pouring in from the window, which meant it was time to get up. He looked at his watch.

Twelve o'clock in the afternoon! The night before, the music had gone on until nearly three in the morning. Mr. Bombompsky was the kind to clean up at the start, so he had only gone to bed at four.

He went to his closet and put on his robe. With the warmth on, he walked to the bathroom and splashed cool water on his face. He shivered, and then was truly awake. Today, he would really have to pack for Marseille.

Mr. Bombompsky took out his blue rolling duffel. He put in two sweaters, four long sleeve button down shirts, two t-shirts, two shorts, two short pants, two long pants, his underwear, and socks. He ran down the stairs and retrieved his Birkenstocks and sneakers. He ran back up and stuffed the shoes into the side pocket of the duffel. He closed his eyes and smiled.

He looked back at his packing. Shirts were sticking out, the shoes created lumps in the pockets, and half a pant leg was hanging out of the bag, flickering in the wind coming from the window. Mr. Bombompsky sighed, covered his eyes with his hands, and fell down on the bed. He was going to Marseille, France, because he wanted to see one of his favorite authors (and mentor) give a talk on one of his latest books. The book he would talk about was called "No Squares." The non-fiction book gave an opinion on how different cultures of the world shouldn't be judged by just a sole group of people. Robert P. Goldman, the author, had gone around the world interviewing people about what stereotypes were common in their country.

Mr. Bombompsky didn't just know of people, but he made contact with them. Two autumns ago, Mr. Bombompsky had heard that Robert Goldman was in New York. Somehow, he found out that Mr. Goldman was going to Central Park on the first Saturday of his stay. Mr. Bombompsky had wanted to meet him, so he made his way from Brooklyn to the city.

"Excuse me, but I think I recognize you," Mr. Bombompsky had planned to say, in a casual tone to get the conversation started. But it had gone the opposite as planned.

Mr. Bombompsky did recognize Mr. Goldman; he was sitting on the bench near the Broadway entrance. Before he could say anything, however, Mr. Goldman exclaimed, "I think I recognize you. Are you, ah, I can't remember!"

Mr. Bombompsky was taken aback, but then knew what Mr. Goldman was going to say. He would have suggested the idea for him, but wanted Mr. Goldman to say it in his own words.

"Oh, oh yes! You are, you are Bombompksy, Mr. Bombompsky the famous writer! Voila! Oh, I have heard so much about you and read all of your books, even the ones for children. It is a pleasure to meet you." He shook Mr. Bombompsky's hand vigorously.

Mr. Bombompsky smiled, very full with satisfaction but trying not to show it too much. A famous writer! Him? Me? He thought. He was being called a well-known author when the true writer was right next to him! But he wondered why Mr. Goldman, who didn't have a French appearance, a French name or last name at all, had a French accent.

"Thank you. And you are Robert Goldman, no? It is a pleasure. Why are you in New York? And where did you come from?" Mr. Bombombpsky had inquired.

"I was recently in Paris," he said while smiling, and the corners of his white mustache lifted up. "I just wanted to explore 'The City,' as they call it, no?"

The conversation was taken to the Tea Lounge, where each of the authors got an espresso. As he thought back to that conversation, Mr. Bombompsky realized he was in no mood to travel, and wished he could hear the conference through his Apple MacBook Air, recorded. But he knew he couldn't let down his old friend. Mr. Bombompsky slowly finished packing the bag, until it closed without anything sticking out.

He went to the bathroom and hopped into the shower. Unintentionally, he turned on the cold water and shrieked. Then he laughed, and soon the cool water began to soothe his body, began to freshen him, began giving him more strength, making him feel lighter: free, like a bird, soaring through the rain, as music began to play in his head as if part of a movie. The rain poured and poured and poured on him, coming out of the hose strongly but making gentle drops of water run down his back. He felt memories flowing through him as the water flowed on his body. He started to imagine himself as a five year old boy, so long ago, when he was afraid of the shower, and wondered how he had come up to having this body, this mind.

That body was still part of him, as were his years of 6, 7, 8, 9, and so on. The water flowed, as he remembered himself throughout his life, as a ten year old, playing soccer, writing, going on vacation, and other things. He, then, was still himself now.

CHAPTER EIGHT

Let the Boy Scream!

"PASTA ODER HUHNCHEN, MISS?"

"Excuse me?" Ida looked up to see another interrupting stewardess.

"Pasta or chicken dinner? Which one would you like?" the stewardess repeated.

"Pasta, thank you," she replied.

The woman took a tray from the cart, put a mini salad on it, a small roll, some butter, a little cup of chocolate pudding, and the hot container of pasta and gave it to Ida.

"Enjoy your meal," she said, and with a lot of enthusiasm, did a little curtsy and skipped on to the next customer.

As she took her first bite of the penne in spicy tomato sauce, Ida heard a big cry. She looked around and saw a toddler sitting two rows away from her stamping his foot and screeching.

Ida shuffled through her bag and found her soundproof headphones. She put them on, and the padding surrounded her; her body was a cloud, she was floating. A Mozart piece began with the deep notes, the one part where the F note was played in each scale, in each minor, in each major; the sad tune played in a dreamy though sharp staccato-legato, the loud chord to the quiet but thoughtful one. It overtook her, to the sky, the surreal sky, and it was quiet; there was no crying baby.

Unfortunately, that was just a daydream. The baby screeched! It screamed, again and again and again, until all the snoring of the double-decker plane had stopped. Ida pressed her earphones closer to her head.

"Where is the siren coming from?"

"What is going on?"

"What is happening?"

"Is there a fire?"

"Will someone turn off that alarm?"

The baby wailed and wailed until it was a whale, a whale getting captured! The baby screamed, louder and louder! The enormously beautiful whale was now harpooned, and vermillion red, crimson, scarlet blood rolled over the waves, signaling that it was fully captured.

The whale song was angry: it sirened a hideous sound: the toddler yelled with rage.

Ida took her wool socks from her bag and put them over the headphones. For a second, it was quiet. She could hear only the ocean waves, a soothing sound—but then a scream! The whale was being turned into oil, its fate was to rule pollution, form into gas, to ruin the world.

The baby threw himself to the aisle of the plane and kicked. Hollering to someone, he banged his whole body against the floor. The sharks were surrounding him, the sweet whale song could not make them leave, and the sound of their teeth chomping over and over again hurt, like a pang of sadness; a horrible fate. They grinded their teeth again and again: From the whale's perspective, the fight had already been fought, and he was to lose, but to the sharks, it had only just begun.

A holler filled the plane: the flesh had been bit, ripped; maroon, magenta, hot red blood came out once again, unable to hold back, just gushing out, coming out by the second, screaming! The fierce sailors on the Nantucket tried to work as quickly as possible to bring the whale up, while trying to stay away from the scavenging sharks who were not only fighting against the whale but against the sailors. There were multiple fights going on at once; between the greed of the men and the sharks, between the desperate innocent whale and its predators!

The harpoon started to loosen as the shark came so very close to eating one of the men, but then it tightened, squeezing the blue life out of the whale, as the men began to regain their strength.

The screaming quieted, and the oil had run out. The snores came back. Ida took off her earphones, mittens, and wool socks.

She herself felt ill, realizing what had just happened. The little boy sat on his mothers lap, taking deep breaths, still showing that ferocious look of torment. The screeching once again went through Ida's body, a sensation—trying to say something. Trying to realize reality as what it is, not what it should be, not what it shouldn't do. The screeching flowed through her body, and as she realized what it did mean, it became softer and quieter, it adjusted and so did she.

As this went through her mind, Mozart came back. The music played, in a way of warmth, of comfort, until the part of the scale, with sharps and flats, when the hand flew through across the notes; playing with all emotions, with anger, sadness, torment, hatred, happiness, stupidity, and loneliness.

Ida had played that scale with all these emotions; all at once and separately. Now the music played with all these feelings, but towards the boy, not for herself. She knew that crying was only asking for something, or getting out the anger of what wasn't happening.

The altered feelings across the plane gradually withered up into a leaf that dropped off a vine and slowly fell to the ground. Headphones went back on, people brought out books, computers, iPods, and drawing pads. The sudden burst of emotion meant nothing now; that past was over, not to be thought about anymore. The memory would stay with the parents, because of their embarrassment, and in Ida's mind as an expressed feeling of a child.

But there that moment lay, in the graveyard of dead moments, of dead history, of the unconscious forgotten stories of the world, of humans, animals, science, all from the big bang, even the unknown from before, to now, to the future forever. The moment lay in the section of minutes, not of seconds, hours, days, weeks, months, years, decades, or centuries. All the forgotten moments; forgotten by most, lay there, unraveling the ribbon of time, of the infinite moments. There also was a memory section. The sad memories sulked. The happy and thoughtful ones didn't take being there for granted, they were happy they had been lived, unlike some of there cousins or brothers and sisters, who had been forgotten right at birth, when any kind of accident or loss occurred, where no one dared to remember.

The music faded, the moments faded, into a mist, but a mist of color, and not forgotten mist, not waste away mist, just put aside mist: mist to think about later. With that thought in mind, Ida opened the book.

CHAPTER NINE

To Write is to Be

THE GENTLE, GENUINE, DELICIOUS, cool, wet, thoughtful rain stopped when Mr. Bombompsky turned the faucet off. The thoughts stopped, the words stopped, so he turned the knob back on. His life flowed through him once again.

When he did get out, he went down stairs and made himself a cup of chai tea. With the hot drink and the refreshed feeling in tow, he went back to his desk and began to write.

Δ Δ Δ

The next morning, Lee Cot awoke to the burning, blazing sun shining onto him. As he got up his eyes looked around and he could see the siltstone, mudstone, and shale on the mountain around him. He thought about all the millions of years it had taken for this to form.

And what about the mountain he was going to? The Mountain of Life? Did that mountain know in the beginning, millions of years ago, what a hit it would be in the future? And just what part of the Mountain's story was Lee; just what part did he take?

He rubbed his eyes and welcomed a new day; a new, action packed day.

Or so he thought.

Or so he wanted.

Or so he feared.

Or so he didn't know.

He stood up, brushing the grains of pale sand off his pants and shirt. He gently rubbed his horse, and with a "neigh", the horse awoke.

Lee Cot looked around, waiting for something to happen. You see, he wasn't sure how the battles he was going to have with Sir E. Vil were going to play out. He'd heard that they would have four major battles, each representing an element of life. But he knew nothing else.

Pushing the thought out of his mind, Cot mounted his horse, patted its mane, and galloped forward.

Δ Δ Δ

Hot tea ran through Mr. Bombompsky's body. The liquid burned him as he thought about the man in black. All his synapses were firing. He was now getting closer to a personal truth, the place where fiction always says something about an author.

He remembered what his parents had told him about living in Portugal before the revolution, during the dictatorship. Spies were watching them wherever they went, watching every move they made. The spy could be a neighbor, a teacher, a doctor, everyone, anyone, and no one could confide in another.

Sir E. Vil was no ordinary man: no ordinary "dressed in black" villain. He represented all the spies, led by the dictator who had controlled his population through fear. In his writing, Mr. Bombompsky would relive, rethink his life through his fiction. Throughout his life, he had realized everything was fiction. The world was created by a fiction. He was created by a fiction—fiction and the real.

Mr. Bombompsky's grandfather had been turned in by his neighbor to the secret police for playing his violin and dancing at two o'clock in the morning. His grandfather was only dancing and playing music because it was his passion, and the only time he had was at night. His dreams came true in the night. When the moon and stars were out, that was his day.

As Mr. Bombompsky reflected on this, he again felt how important it was for him to write. It was important for every person to have a love. He did have a girlfriend once. But on their third date, the girl never showed up, and Mr. Bombompsky decided love was not for him. His characters had become his children, because he had so much love for them. In a way, they were biological because many of them were inspired from his own life.

His past, present, and thoughts on the future had always made a huge impact on his books. Mr. Bombompsky stuck his pencil into the electric sharpener. He could hear the lead being sliced off, coming to a point, the past life of the pencil slicing off and falling into darkness. He quickly pulled it out, and felt the sharp pointy tip, replenished, reborn, and ready. Mr. Bombompsky had to figure out a way for Lee Cot to get the treasure. His mind started working again, and it became very clear.

CHAPTER TEN

I Give You Superman

THE WHOLE DAY COT traversed through whirling canyons, darting through the desert. The sand storms were strong, and though he couldn't quite see where he was going, his horse somehow led him. He came upon mountain after mountain, cliff after cliff, dune after dune.

Then he saw it: a grand, steep structure. It was tall, taller then tall! It had enormous volume, beautifully curved edges, and from a certain vantage he could truly see; it was alive. He had reached the Mountain of Life.

Cot put his hand on his head. He stepped off his horse.

Cot put his head on his hand. He horsed off his step.

He blinked. What?

What Lee Cot was experiencing now was the feeling of uncertainty, of confusion. It was a puzzling moment, right then. For it was the start of something great, of something wonderful and futuristic!

But Cot didn't know what to make of it. He didn't know how to seize the moment!

Cot wiped his brow and sneered. "This is not a book. This is real life. I can do this. Of course I can. I have to! All I'm doing is pursuing my life. This is what I'm doing. God, get on with it, man! There is no pen about to scribble your next move. You're not a story! You yourself are going to control what is about to happen! So do it!"

And at that moment, that "ugh!" moment, was when Lee Cot put one foot in front of the other, put one breath after another, put spirit, soul, and energy into the moment, put his very mind into what he was about to do, despite the fact he had no idea what was going to happen.

Also at that moment, coincidentally, the action began.

Lee Cot charged on his horse up the base of the mountain, forgetting about the heat and the stress and the pain and the confusion. He went farther and farther, not thinking but just moving, moving, moving up, up, up! He zoomed into the horizon, making a wild shadow in the brilliant colors of the sunset. He excitedly pounded up on the dirt, ran up on the path, trying to get further and further, slithering his way up this so-called "mountain."

He galloped furiously into the future, up the mountain, up up up! He could feel gravity leaving him, he could feel that feeling of flying, of soaring through time and being! He felt it all!

From a cave far away, though in the same desert, a man sat down on a mat and scribbled something into a notebook. The man looked through his telescope up to a mountain where he surprisingly saw something moving quickly. The faint outline portrayed a human on some sort of running animal. The man knew who this was. He knew exactly who he was and why and where and how he was doing this.

But he acted like an innocent stranger.

It's amazing, what emotions can do to a man. See, this man knew positively well that no one was watching him, but nevertheless he still got that feeling that someone could see him. Despite this worry, he chewed on the eraser of his pencil and once again wrote something in his journal:

Day 1: Lee Cot has approached the Mountain, and with much courage it appears he is brave enough to get a head start on climbing it. He's a darn valiant boy, clearly. But he's going to tire out and Sir E. Vil will, with no doubt, be ahead of him in no time.

The stranger closed his book. He smiled, and then proceeded to snicker.

"What a game," he thought, "What a silly, useless game."

Meanwhile, Lee Cot scampered up through the mountain, hoping to get somewhere. Had he known a spy from the Bad World was watching him at the moment, he would have been much more careful. But Cot, at the moment, did not know.

Out of breath, Cot stopped his horse and yawned. He rubbed his eyes wearily. Cot found a decent spot on the earthy ground and lay down for a moment, sighing again and again.

He thought. He thought about thinking. Then he realized that he should be thinking about something useful.

Now what would be useful in this kind of situation? That's not a statement, it's a question! Huh? Well, Cot didn't know either.

Until a moment later, that is. He should practice his skills, he thought. He would need to have some backup plans for the battles.

You would think that Cot would know more about the battles than he did, but he didn't! All he knew was the outline of what was to happen, no details whatsoever.

So with this pursuit, Cot began to think of what he was good at. He certainly didn't have any weapons; he knew that for a fact. And he hoped Sir E. Vil didn't either.

So he thought and thought. At one point he was so fed up with thinking that he just began to do something.

He took a handful of sand and threw it at a nearby tree. The sand swooshed about, hitting the tree and it's surroundings. Not bad, he thought.

Next, he took a big, thick stick and attempted to break it. On the first try, it went "crack!"

Preceding that, Lee Cot took another stick and aimed for a low hanging branch not too far away from him. The wood went flying in the air but missed the branch. Cot groaned.

Even after multiple throws, he missed again and again.

Little did he know, the man was watching Lee Cot. In his notebook he wrote:

Lee Cot - Strengths: sand throws?, strong arms, is skilled at breaking things. Weaknesses: terrible aim.

Back on the mountain, Cot heard a scream. It was a low pitched, rumbling voice that echoed throughout the desert. Cot immediately jerked his head, in search of the culprit.

But as soon as his face turned around he saw a fluttering cape, a frightening grimace in the distance. It was Sir E. Vil. It was scary, though kind of cool! Evil had a face.

But it was too late. The first battle of the elements, Earth, had begun.

Dirt, gravel, and sand came flinging at him! All at once they hit his body, pounding against him.

In shock, Cot didn't know what to do.

Avalanches came rolling down the mountain, hitting him, slapping him! All the parts of the Earth came down on him all at once! It was a sand storm, with the little grains flying about everywhere, as well as an Earth storm, with trees falling down and sticks breaking and nature screaming!

It was beautifully, scarily, amazingly frightening! Here all the elements of Earth, all the forces of Earth were painfully against him, yet it was stunning!

But then, right then, Cot took action. His face was a lantern, glowing with light and anger and power. He roared, running like the wind in his enemy's direction, tearing the ground as he went. He screamed with all his might, crunched his fist, and punched the air! As soon as he did this a whole tree went falling on Sir E. Vil, pushing him to the ground in an instant. As he punched the tree swayed, smacking Vil in every which way!

It was so, so dominating, so prevailing, so compelling, yet so daunting!

Then, Sir E. Vil crawled out from under the tree, picked it up with his bare arms and his super-human strength, and you could see the white of his knuckles, the anger in his face, and the determination in him as he threw it powerfully in Cot's direction. Cot was too shocked to take action. But it seemed that his consciousness took action for him.

He put his hands in front of him, and when the tree came his way he caught it, grabbing it with his rough, potent hands, and with his strong, mighty fingers he broke the tree trunk in half and threw it back to Sir E. Vil.

Then, quickly as can be, he grabbed handfuls and handfuls of dirt and sand and threw them consistently at Vil, who suffered the smack of pain at its entirety.

Cot's head began to pound! The Earth rumbled beneath him, shaking, shaking.

He screamed once again like a maniac, feeling outrageous and significant! He was kicking ass.

And yet he didn't know what had taken over him, he didn't know what he had just done!

But he had done something in his favor. And with the screams of pain from both contestants, Cot realized he had won the first battle, and was 25% closer to the future being in his hands (did I mention he's good at math?).

Δ Δ Δ

I sighed, smiling so hard and staring at the crisp, yellow drafting paper with words everywhere.

Δ Δ Δ

Power, strength—super human strength: Mr. Bombompsky read and reread the passage while thinking about whether this was what he wanted Lee Cot to be like. Was he really a magic cowboy? Was he really a superhero? Would he be a super hero? How could he go from a western cowboy to a cosmic, telekinetic magician on a horse? That made no sense, or whatever sense meant. What was the story, really? What was the plot?

But could Lee Cot get rid of the dictatorship? Would it bring back happiness to his parents? If fiction could solve all those things...

Emil's imagination had taken over him and Mr. Bombompsky. His head began to hurt. It was outrageously unrealistic. But why did it have to be realistic? Did it, even? Mr. Bombompsky plopped his head down on his desk, unsure what to do, unsure what to feel. If only he could snap and his teacup would instantly be refilled and he would be in a hot, bubbling bath. So much thought had been put in; but it just wasn't right. Was it the writer's obligation to keep the reader in the real, or in the right genre?

Mr. Bombompsky remembered back to his elementary school days; learning about fiction, nonfiction, fantasy, biographies, and all the other genres. It all came back to him in a flash; when he was very young and in an E.L.A. class, writing a historical essay on one of the early explorers, and he wrote that the sailor sailed over the moon. The next day, his teacher asked to meet with him after class. She told him that sailors don't sail over the moon, only over the sea. "This sailor has strange and magical powers! It's just a figure of speech," he had said earnestly. His teacher looked at him very puzzlingly, and explained that speech and words referred only to real things. But Mr. Bombompsky just knew that couldn't be real. This could not be true: Words could have many magical powers and meanings. Each word could create a world, move people, countries, and make horses fly. Words weren't things, but they certainly had powers.

In any event, Mr. Bombompsky had always let imagination take over what was real to him, and at this moment he wondered why that was.

Fiction could change the world, maybe, but it would be his only world that was changed. If every character was a part of their author, Lee Cot was part of Mr. Bombompsky.

Mr. Bombompsky wondered who he was, and who his author was.

Emil was writing Lee Cot, so it was Emil who would have to be changed. When Mr. Bombompsky was little, and even now, he and his friends had created huge fantasy tales, plays, war games with flying horses, and even make something up for a school writing project. He had taken so much pleasure in coming up with the stories. So he knew how Emil felt.

Emil and his writing of Lee Cot were made up by Mr. Bombompsky, and Mr. Bombompsky wanted magic; but magic in a sense that is believable only if you believe. All of what could (or would) happen to Lee Cot could happen to anyone who wanted it too; it could happen to someone who understands the meaning of the real. Real didn't have to be or not be.

Mr. Bombompsky felt power and strength running through him again.

"It wasn't real or not real, forget about real," he thought. "Think about what you put into the real, what you can, will, and do make real. Go fly across the Atlantic Ocean. Do it. Oh, it's not believable? Well, have you ever tried?!"

As Mr. Bombompsky talked back and forth with himself in his mind, he felt all the reassurance come back, all his pencils ready to bullet. He put his hands over his face, not sure whether to be angry or to smile. More, more, he thought, do it before Marseille. He ripped an empty sheet out of his sketchpad, and started drawing and jotting down words, pictures, and sentences. When he was angry, pushing himself, he pushed the lead to make a deep, thick line. Some sketches where light as a feather, some thick, some thin. He drew circles, squares, and vases. He drew his feelings, he wrote what he needed to express. He thought about his life; thought about his earlier years, his previous books, all the newspaper articles and books he had read, and all his mentor authors. He made lines of squiggles, a small sketch of a violin, and words that came to his mind. He decided he wouldn't start Cot all over, and just continue the battles from where he had left off. Mr. Bombompsky would make some thing good out of it; that was for sure. He drew some more, and when he felt ready, when all his emotions had fled, he went back to his writing.

Δ Δ Δ

While all this action was taking place, the man with the notepad had a puzzled look on his face. He was absolutely confused about what had just happened.

Now this man, being the angry though insightful man he was, began to sing a song. He always did this when things where troubling him.

He took a breath, put a frown on his face, and started spinning.

*"What is happening? What is happening? What am I doing? What what
what what?*

*What I just saw with my two honest eyes was something I've never seen
before... what I just saw with my two honest eyes, was something I'd like to
see more. Even though it was hideous, hideous and frightening, it was quite:
quite amazing as well!*

*You see I... have... lived on the bad side of the world for as long as I can
remember. Since I was a baby, since I was born, I have never, never really,
really mourned! But now, the good is overpowering the evil! Lee Cot and Sir
E. Vil are fighting each other and Lee Cot is winning, oh my! Lee Cot, as
you might of assumed, is from the good .... side. Sir E. Vil, as you might of
assumed, is from the bad .... side! And I don't know what to make of it.
What have these separations, separations of 'good' and 'bad', done to us?*

*I'm questioning my life. I'm questioning my job. I'm questioning the whole
entire system of belief!*

*You see I came here... as a spectator... to keep track... of the battles... of
Cot and Vil. I was supposed to. Supposed to do that. I was supposed to be on
the bad side; I was supposed to be rooting for the Evil. I was supposed to take
notes on both contestants. I was supposed to make sure... that the period got
placed on the Mountain of Life!*

But now, now, now, now, I'm not sure if I'm going to do what I was supposed to.

After all? I don't know any after all!

It's only been one day! It's only been one battle! It's only been one section of the journey!

And I've already made an assssssssssummmmmmp-ttiiiiiionnnnn. But what if my assssssssssummmmmmp-ttiiiiiionnnnn proves wrong?

I must look like a goofball standing here, spinning around, and screaming against my will!

But the strange thing is, I don't care about that! I'm just, I'm just, I'm just trying to figure a few things out!"

Wow! That was some expression.

The man flopped down onto the sandy ground. He moaned, complaining to the air. What he was facing was the struggle of realization. He was not a typical character from a good-VS-evil story. He was a man! He was a person! He *is* a man; he *is* a person!

And at that moment, he fiddled with his own personal perception; and wondered what to believe, what to hope for, what to want at that very moment.

Was Cot going to win? Was Sir E. Vil going to win? What was the future?

That night the sky was piercing, and it seemed all of eternity was looking down at Lee, with the bright, star-shaped embers in the sky.

The night was lit up, not by a campfire, but by the millions of fireballs in the sky, millions of light years away.

Cot thought, "Who am I? Which fireball am I?"

But he knew, he and the stars were one. And that if he could just draw on this force of power he would get through the next battle.

Δ Δ Δ

Ida rubbed her intrigued eyes that did not want to leave the page.

"Meine Damen und Herren, wie viele von Ihnen wissen, hat es, und noch immer vor sich geht, eine riesige Waldbrand in Berlin. Es war viel länger als erwartet anhaltende und durch große Brände, werden wir nicht in der Lage, zu landen."

Ida heard everyone groan. She knew, even though she did not understand what was being said, that it wasn't good. From the speaker, she heard the pilot sigh and then continue on.

"Wenn Sie die Turbulenz bemerkt haben, haben wir in den letzten 20 Minuten lang kreisen, und wir sind jetzt sehr kurz auf Gas. Wir landen in Wroclaw, Polen sehr kurz sein. Wir freuen uns sehr leid für die Verspätung, aber das ist nicht unsere Verantwortung. Wenn wir landen, an die zwei Schreibtische gegenüberliegenden Seite des Gepäckband gehen. Das Management dort wird Sie mit allem, Wohnen, Essen, und dem nächsten Flug zu helfen. Auch hier sind wir sehr bedauern und hoffen, Sie werden es sicher wieder machen. "

"Ladies and gentlemen, as many of you know, the enormous forest fire in Berlin continues. It has been ongoing for much longer than expected, and due to this we will not be able to land. If you have noticed the turbulence, we have been circling for the past 20 minutes, and are now very low on fuel. We will be landing in Wroclaw, Poland very shortly. We are very sorry for the delay, but this is not our responsibility. When we land, go to the two desks opposite side of the baggage carousel. The airline personnel will be able to help you with everything: rebooking, housing, food, the next flight, and everything you need. Again, we are very sorry and hope you will make it back safely."

CHAPTER ELEVEN

Lost in Flight

IDA'S MOUTH SLOWLY FELL open, and then her jaw slammed
back up. Ida had always seen actors do this in movies, and for a period
earlier in her life she had been fascinated with the movement. She had
rehearsed it many times, and, she decided, this was the perfect time to
play the role.

But this wasn't just acting. This was going the wrong way, the right
way to somewhere else, and that somewhere else was the opposite
direction from her home. Wide eyed and with a sigh, she looked
around the plane at all the other faces and expressions that had over
taken the sky. Some people were shaking there heads and sighing, some
had hands slapped over their faces, the very quick and intuitive people
were already searching for a hotel on their phones and scribbling
numbers down, and then there were the kids, who were just as happy
as they had been three and a half minutes ago, playing games, reading,
or watching something.

When she was in these kind of situations, Ida tried to use logic and
equations to find a solution. Like: when she was on a train leaving
Grand Central Station, and the train was not moving because it had no
conductor. He was with his wife who was having a baby. That part she

figured out: the city was having some problems. If the MTA staff of New York City couldn't figure out that people shouldn't board the train if there was no conductor, they were the Small Apple with a worm in it.

She shook her head, wondering if that equation was nonsense, or if she was just trying to be funny, or if it actually helped: which, she thought, how could it? This plane, full of frustrated passengers, equaled not a problem, but a state of life. People could stomp around and sulk in their heads, but they couldn't do anything about Mother Nature. The reasonable thing to think about was why Father Nature was not helping. If tornadoes and hurricanes were happening, shouldn't the husband try to calm down the wife? But then, if the husband and wife are having an argument, then the child, (the storm), has a reason to get mad, and burst out into tears (rain). But the parents of the storm don't realize that their child is causing an extreme disturbance to another universe. If they were made with any sense at all, they would know what was causing their rain and storms, and they might figure out that they are the cause of someone else's. If everything was a universe in itself, then one stomp could affect everything.

Something struck Ida. She winced, and deep, dark piano notes began to tremble and stomp. Suddenly, the next scale was playing an angry melody, just two notes being beaten. The music moved one scale up, and the three chords that began to play were enough to scare an adult who is usually scared of nothing. The music shifted up and up to the ongoing scales, playing frightful, horribly sad and emotional sounds. The storm of notes was taking over her mind. The first lightning bolt struck when the last note on the left side of the piano was played. It hurt, it was a huge scrape with no band-aid, no Neosporin, and no love that would make it heal. In her mind, Ida saw the ship, rocking quickly against the harsh waves, shaking and braking in half. Then she saw him falling off the ship, and she heard something being muttered in polish, "Kocham cie Id- ". That was all that was heard.

Ida quickly pushed the image out of her mind. Or at least she tried to. Poland, where her husband had died in a tempest, was not even the right way to somewhere else, it was the way to sadness.

She tried to push that thought out of her mind again, but it wouldn't budge. Someone, something wanted her to think about it. She tried to dump the whole feeling to where it belonged: forgotten. Though maybe, she realized with a classic da, da, da, from the piano, she was meant to remember.

Ida furiously started to try to think about something else; something that was the opposite of death. She scribbled down notes in her book, calculating costs, distances, places, and how she might get home. Anything: She would do anything keep death out of her mind.

They did say they would take care of it all, she thought. Even though a very minor (sad) note played, she was still happy with her discovery.

She did know, however, that this could not possibly be all true, but she let it deceive her for the moment: "we will take care of it all." But, but, but what did that expression mean? She thought helplessly.

She tried to open her book and read, but could only stare at each word, and wonder who had the energy to write them. She kept on thinking, until a light flickered on in front of her. It was the fasten-your-seat-belt sign, and it meant that they were landing.

She tidied up her papers and put them all in her bag. She could feel the warmth of the clouds as the plane flew down through them. Trying to bring up her own spirit, she closed her eyes and hummed "home" in the way that yogis say "ohm," even though she was far from home. "Why not be an optimist?" she muttered with a snicker. The plane was a bird, soaring down, going down to his family after a long journey. The bird gently flew down, through the clouds seemed to capture it, but with a bit of struggle, it kept on going. Down and down, wanting badly to see its mate again. It flew, but then it crashed.

The plane came to a rough stop.

Even with its half injured wing, it had to get home and see its family. Slowly, the helpless though determined bird flapped to the tree where it had lived numerous years ago. Its sister and mother were quietly weeping, and right before its eyes was a very injured wing, that sadly, was connected to a dead body. Ida groaned. Why was she forced to think about this?

The plane slowly came to a stop. After minutes of waiting, the seatbelt light went off, and the unbuckling was a wave across the double-decker plane. Ida walked along the hall and came to the door.

"Danke," said a stewardess waiting at the doorway. Ida didn't even fake a smile.

As she approached the main room of the airport, she noticed a Help Desk and proceeded to walk in its direction.

After waiting in line for quite a few minutes, Ida finally was in front of it.

"Yes, may I help you?" the woman said in a very unusual and squeaky voice.

"Well, what should I do?"

"About what?" The woman said with a puzzled look on her face, although Ida new that she knew exactly what the problem was.

"Oh!" She said like it was the most obvious thing in the world.

"Oh yes." She nodded her head with her eyes closed and her mouth in a very fake sympathetic way. "So, we have two flights back to Germany, specifically Frankfurt and Berlin, next Saturday. The smoke cover from the fire is still quite bad, and we are still waiting to hear when we can fly next. But we do have flights departing to Canada! Is the US your final destination?"

"Yes," Ida said slowly.

"Oh! Well then, the next flight to Montreal is in two weeks, and I am sure there is a flight from there to...?"

"New York," Ida said, though not satisfied with this idea.

"Yes, New York! The city! Marvelous!" The woman looked dreamily around the room. Then a small snarl came across her face. " Yes, anyway. You may find the flight on our website, PolishAirlines.com. Thank you. A good something to do while your waiting is have a Polish coffee at Dunkin Doughnuts. Oh, in New York don't they have Broadway?! And the Statue of Liberty? Oh, oh my, the wonders of the city! Oh yes, baby... Next!" She gave Ida a slight push and moved her out of the way.

Ida looked up at the woman, who was completely ignoring her, with a look that even she couldn't describe herself. Though as she looked around the whole airport, Ida saw a Dunkin Doughnuts, just like the woman had said, a Burger King, and a pop-up Target: she wasn't so sure about these Poles. Ida picked herself up and walked again to the end of the line.

After waiting another ten minutes and getting nowhere, Ida decided to...

She didn't decide to do anything. What if someone, an author, was writing her, and that book had already been published and now someone was reading her. Maybe she was living a book. So if she couldn't find anything to do, or didn't decide anything, her reader would probably skip the book and move on.

Her mind suddenly was a fire, tears streaming down her face, the ocean about to explode. This time, no piano music was there to make it gentler, she was just burning and hurting. She put her sweaty hands to her face, and quietly in a whisper, mumbled to herself, "No, no, no. Stop it. What have I done to myself: what have I done?" Her husband's voice suddenly muttered a loud whisper in her mind, and this was not a Shakespearean tragedy, this was not acting, this was really happening now, to her. The fire, the tempest, the piano were all real to her in her mind, real to her at this moment in future history.

It all came out in a way that it was screaming, begging, pleading to go back to its hiding shell, never wanting to come out. "Who am I?" she thought, as she took a high breath, not a deep one. She suddenly had a flash back of when she was seven, and she watched a TV show called, Me, Eloise. She had loved it, and though she didn't now how, she had been Ida's role model as a seven year old. Eloise would always say "I'm Eloise, who are you?" So Ida was Ida, but who was the Ida that was Ida? And what the layers were beneath that, she had not the slightest idea.

It all came out in a way that it was screaming, begging, pleading to go back to its hiding shell, never wanting to come out. "Who am I?" she thought, as she took a high breath, not a deep one. "Who am I, why am I here? Am I supposed to be here? Was I an accident? Am I a product of nature, of life?"

Ida was Ida, but who *was* the Ida that was Ida? And what the layers were beneath that, she had not the slightest idea.

Than her adult mind overtook the others and whispered, "This is the wrong time for this." But Ida thought to herself, when was the right time? The right time was when these feelings came out, when they where vivid, and that was now. She was in an airport she had never been before, let alone heard about. She had nowhere to go, no room service and no hot tub, no bed nor bathroom, even though those sheepish liars on the plane had said she would. And most of all, she had no one.

CHAPTER TWELVE

The Coffee Shop

THE SMELL OF HOT bean coffee filled her nostrils, and this smell she liked. She turned around, and instead of Dunkin Doughnuts, she saw Cremchanksavich Kaffe. She gasped. Her name was Polish? Maybe she was meant to be here. Her senses then returned, and she went to the shop and got herself a treat.

An hour later, while Ida was still at the café, the announcement that flights to Berlin were cleared came, and that they would be boarding any minute. She felt a sudden thrill and a rush of extreme happiness go through her mind.

Twenty minutes later, Ida Cremchanskivich was sitting in first class on her way home. Oh, so much for happy endings.

Ida tried to think about something. She tried to think about her music, she tried thinking about her past, her hopes for the future, the book she was reading and so on. One could say that because she was not succeeding in thinking straight about something, she was thinking about nothing at all. But what she was really thinking about was *thinking about* thinking. Thinking, thinking, thinking. She said this word a few times, and then it started to sound strange. That word was chosen for its meaning for a reason. And that reason was chosen for some other reason.

Deep in the bag was the book that was about to tell the truth, to reveal the answer to her question. That book was just waiting to be read by someone who could understand it. That book was waiting, feeling audacious, ready to share its magic that was thoroughly real. And at that very moment, the book was taken into hands, and the hands turned the page; the eyes moved, reading.

CHAPTER THIRTEEN

The Battle of Fire

THE NEXT DAY CAME quickly. Something felt blurry; like Cot couldn't really see. But the thing he wasn't seeing was himself.

He was amazed at what he had done the other day. He was appalled at his super-strength, and his ability to, well, to win!

It felt uncontrollable. Lee Cot was mystified.

Suddenly, Cot heard music. Loud, adventurous, theme-song music. Bum bum bum bum bum bum bum bum bum bum bum bum bum bum bum bum bum bum bum bum bum bum bum bum bum bum bum bum bum bum bum bum bum bum bum bum bum bum bum bum bum bum bum bum bum bum bum bum bum.

And then BAM! The second battle, Fire, had begun.

Fireballs came flying in Lee Cot's direction, just like he had envisioned the night before. These were shooting stars, catapulting towards him. If the battle of Earth would bury him and overwhelm him, the battle of fire would singe him and burn him in an instant.

He had to get over this fear.

Before he could think, flame emerged from every tree surrounding him. Everything began to burn.

Blurs of orange, red and yellow were all he could see. The heat was suffocating; the smoke billowing and choking him. Fire flickered in every which way. It was even as if his mind was burning. It was so sudden Cot didn't have enough time to take it all in.

But then, Cot noticed Sir E. Vil standing on a hill not to far away from him. Of course!

And on that hill, the madman was crackling, snickering, laughing in pure, disgusting delight. It was an awful sight.

Cot just stood there, heavily breathing, glaring at his enemy.

"You," Cot began, screaming. "You are so violent, tricky, devious, sadistic, vicious, cruel, nasty, spiteful, malicious, horrid, unpleasant, repulsive, appalling, dire, terrible, calamitous, dreadful, ruinous, eerie, bamboozling, baffling, though remarkably astonishing! What are you?"

And then, something devastating happened. Lee Cot levitated from the ground, rising higher and higher into the air, above the smoke layer. And soon he was in the white, fluffy layer of clouds. What was he doing here? How did he get up?

Here amongst the clouds he rendered them open and a deluge of water instantly dropped down onto Sir E. Vil. It came down in all forms; in thunder, sleet, snow, rain, hail, lighting.

He had countered fire using the force of water.

He had combined the battle of fire with the battle of water.

But of course! Fire and water were complete opposites, so why not use them together? Together, they are a strong force beyond any other!

Sir E. Vil had flung fire at Cot, but Cot had overpowered him with the power of opposition.

It was a happening metaphor.

When the skies cleared, Lee could see the entirety of the mountain. He felt like he was up on a satellite, like Google Earth looking down. And yet, he was just standing there. But it was as if he could be standing there and at the same time seeing it from high above. Wow. He, his body, whomever he was seemed to be able to move through different forms of energy and matter through time.

Then he imagined himself giving a speech to the whole Good World. People would be cheering, clapping in excitement all for him. But how could he explain what he had just realized? How could any science, how could any logic of language explain these powers that he had felt and come upon and experienced?

That night he felt calm, though knowing at the same time that maybe the biggest battle was ahead of him.

That was why he had to get that question mark on top of the Mountain. He had to let the human race know that they had extraordinary powers, because they did! And while it was something that no one had ever realized before, Lee Cot would be the one to share it.

Surely he couldn't be beaten in this last battle! He could win!

Is this all a dream? He thought. Will I make it?

And that was for him to find out the very next day.

Δ Δ Δ

Humming happily, Mr. Bombompsky opened his laptop. He just looved unfinished endings. They led to millions of new possibilities.

He clicked on the iTunes tab and chose some music. He put on a song by Air, one he had loved since he was a kid. The music brought many memories to recollection: memories of his childhood. He had always thought of the music as a perfect ending song for a movie, but never had heard used as one.

He listened to the trumpet make a few beats, and then the whole symphony began to play. And then- the rock came. It was the best mixture, he thought. Mr. Bombompsky even put his hands to his chest and pretended to play an air guitar.

He whistled the tune, imagining himself playing all the instruments, in the dreamy way that the music possessed. The musical tone rose higher and higher, the notes forming a mountain, then it got quiet, and the soft waves of the water splashed over the mountain. If this was the theme song for an end of something, then what was the beginning and middle?

The beginning and middle he had already figured out, but what would be Lee Cot's future?

One song, one speech, could posses and represent a whole life. As he listened to the bouncy strings of the electric guitar, he realized those were the bounces of someone's story, the shaking of someone's life, the imagined sounds of dreams. The song easily could be interpreted as melancholy on the outside, as grief, but when going deeper, Mr. Bombompsky found that it had feelings that did not have to do with happy or sad or everyday words. The music was reaching its high point, its moment of triumph and then it slowly melted into a soft liquid chocolate. Then something slurped that chocolate, and the only way to get the delicate sweetness back was to press the play button.

He chose another song by Air. This song was more disguised—something trying to be trying, but not succeeding. The bells in the song chimed, and then a light voice came in and said, "Don't run away from time." The music became darker, deeper. He wanted to speak to the music, to ask it why? What was wrong?

The music filled the house. Mr. Bombompsky couldn't understand it. What was it? What was the music really feeling, if it was feeling anything at all?

So he took out an empty piece of paper and started scribbling so quickly that he made many mistakes. He tried to write the music, the sounds in words, scribbling each note in the way it came out to him. Then, along with the music he heard the faint sound of his pen touching the paper. So he started writing about that.

Then, without pressing any button whatsoever, the song "Don't Stop Believing" by Journey came on. At first, he was so focused on the sound of the pen that he didn't notice. But then the hallucination (or the memory) came, and he was screaming happiness, so was his younger brother, and he was at a rock concert. The music filled his ears, it felt so good, he was being reborn, and with his energy he could overcome and do anything; it was such a nurturing moment!

When he was ten years old, music was his life. He cherished it. So his mother had taken him and his brother to a live concert to see Journey play. And as he remembered this moment, he felt it again. He stood up on his chair, put his hand to his mouth, and became a rock star.

It was the musicality of words. He could now see Lee Cot take flight in his imagination, and what was Lee but the shape and form of his thought, the very energy that this music had pumped and filled him with? Music gave feeling to adventure, to this adventure, and Lee Cot was the adventure of Mr. Bombompsky, never realized. Lee was the braver Bombompsky, the daring, the faster draw on the gun, the quick intuitive instinct, the boy who could take wind and turn it into a sail to soar over the ocean, the warrior who threw the arrow that would always hit the target.

Now Bombompsky was in Lee Cot, and vise versa, too; not just words on a paper.

Δ Δ Δ

When he awoke the next morning, Lee Cot was feeling good. As he drifted into his morning consciousness he felt he was one with time and all the powers of the universe, and he sensed that thinking was an action in itself.

But then, suddenly, his body began to vibrate and shake. The awful feeling came with a sound as well; a horrible, howling sound. It seemed to be that the sky was burping in rage!

The wind became the all mighty god. The thunder cackled with excitement. The air spun around, blowing everything out of its place.

It was the Battle of Wind, of Air.

Wind was a god: Greek, Roman, and everything else.

And yet Sir E. Vil, the man behind all this, had conjured it as if it was his god to do his bidding, to be his weapon, and now he used it to take Lee Cot down.

The wind picked up Lee and his horse and hurled them against the canyon's sandstone rocks, pounding them against the thin, unsteady cliff. A waterfall of stone poured over in front of them. For that single moment, while encapsulated under the pounding rocks he was given shelter and a few seconds to compose himself.

Now, he was going to make his plan to take over that evil.

So what did this evil want, Lee thought. Who was, what was Sir E. Vil; what did he want? Immortality, never ending life, 'enjoyable' life, maybe? Did he want everything like a spoiled child, everything he wanted when he wanted and the way he wanted?

But Lee Cot knew that living, dying, and having un-enjoyable experiences were all part of life.

But what if his rival didn't know that?

Right then the sand covered them completely, causing rocks to hurl down. They flew at him too, because the wind was blowing them everywhere.

What was the opposite of wind? What could Lee Cot do in revenge, having to do with air or wind?

The first thing he thought was to not listen. There would be no sound, there would be no howling, there would be no wind: he would block out all of it. He would close his ears: he would block the universe from all sorts of sounds.

And then, suddenly everything was perfectly quiet, and without the sound he could see; it was simply a wind tornado and swirls of color and energy and stones and sands.

The whooshing of the air had quieted just by his concentration.

So if he concentrated on something without a tornado, maybe the tornado would go away too!

He tried to block away the vision of the tornado. He relaxed his mind and his tense muscles but gripped his horse tightly.

Cot was in a good position, so maybe if he stayed calm and sturdy, Sir E. Vil would tire out.

And that is exactly what happened.

Δ Δ Δ

Mr. Bombompsky caught the numbers on his alarm clock just as the 32 was tingling, transforming, changing into a 33. Lost in thought, he studied the number. The number read: 11:33. Ah, two ones, two threes. One-one-three-three, eleven-thirty-three…

11:33?! The time, just a simple few numbers, struck him like lightning. He was to get up at four in the morning the next day to catch his 6:45 a.m. flight! Mr. Bombompsky started busying himself and telling himself he had to get busy and get to work. He did this, but there was only one problem. He had nothing busy to do.

Then his mind trailed off again, and again, and again, and he thought about how great it would be to swim in a pool of chocolate, and how fondue with strawberry—

"Stop it!" Mr. Bombompsky said aloud. Then he looked around to see who had just said stop it.

"Stop it, Mr. B! You know what your doing. You have got to focus, and stop inventing distractions. Stop. Stop that, and start this." He said to himself.

But start what? Nothing. The whole world of adults, and even young adults, revolved around rushing and whether "something was real or not." What a useless life. When Mr. Bombompsky was a child, he contemplated this many times, and even thought about becoming a human/robot scientist. He had never heard of this profession, just invented this type of science for he thought it was completely and utterly practical and useful. He'd wanted to come up with a solution to this terrible problem by transplanting children's minds into adults.

But I am an adult, he thought. So I should stop being such a stereotype. I, for one, am special! But then how come not everyone is special? Some people are great thinkers, yes. So rest that case.

Mr. Bombompsky went to his bed, fluffed his comforter and crawled in, clothes and all. He was intentionally lying there for his thinking minutes; not to fall asleep, but, in any event, he did, very quickly in fact. So he lay there, gently snoring, emerging into the world of dreams.

CHAPTER FOURTEEN

Hotel Pomegranate

THE BLACK CAR CAME to a halt in front of a tall, gold building, Hotel Pomegranate. The car door opened, and out came a man dressed in a black suit with blue Birkenstocks. He had glasses, a pencil in his ear, and he carried a notebook, a black notebook, with certain words like "fanatic," "beginning," "end," "life," "fire," "soul," "live," and "realism" written in a thick, chalky white on the front cover.

"Ah, Bonjour Monsieur Bombompsky, bienvenue, bienvenue; velcome to zee 'Otel Pomograaaaneete," said another man in a thick, French accent.

"Merci beaucoup, Felix. It is nice to see you again." Replied Mr. Bombompsky in a good attempt of a French accent, while he gave Felix a hug.

He and Felix had met the last time he had come to Marseille, and they had become good friends. Mr. Bombompsky tried to hide a yawn, but it came out very clearly. Felix understood right away, catching one of his own, and immediately accommodated Mr. Bombompsky to his room.

When Mr. Bombompsky arrived at the hotel in Marseille, France, it was already late at night. As soon as he reached his hotel room, he quickly unpacked and ordered a cheese sandwich, some olives, and a glass of red wine through room service. When the food arrived, he sat down at the built in desk and began eating while skimming his notes for the book conference.

As he was rereading the first page of "No Squares," Robert Goldman's book, he heard a small chirp come from outside. He heard it again; it was like a message, calling for him to come. Mr. Bombompsky walked towards the window and opened it. Outside was a small robin, nestled in a tiny nest made of sticks and long grass stems. They were weaved together in a constant pattern, and inside, the bird was hovering over something. It was a baby robin, smaller than two thumbs put together. It was so fresh, so new, so in the process of becoming alive.

Mr. Bombompsky gently stroked its soft feathers. He smiled to the mother bird, and knew that somehow, she could understand him. With a quick, sharp chirp, the bird almost smiled back.

He closed the window, but left a sliver open so he could, in some way, be connected to the bird. This felt necessary.

Mr. Bombompsky threw on his "Mind the Gap" t-shirt from England and some red pajama pants and crawled into bed.

Δ Δ Δ

Three days later, Ida Cremchanskivich found herself on a plane going back to New York. The only problem was that they were flying in the opposite direction. Instead of flying over the Atlantic Ocean, they were flying over Asia and across the Pacific because air traffic was completely closed due to the warning of an impending natural disaster.

She looked out the window and marveled at the extraordinary landscape. How different things looked from up above. The earth was so alive; and it was really being lived. She looked at the gentle roll of the mountains; they were the skin of a body; the clothes of the earth.

And then, just as the fat man—the big man across the isle—with the Pork Pie hat, reading the Financial Times with his tri-focal glasses, in his Hermes tie, eating the last bite of the Coté d'Or chocolate, sipping a glass of gingerale, burped! His hiccup was the very trembling of the earth: The whole world seemed to belch; the plane shook and tilted violently. The earth's hiccup had been too strong; its sickness too ill, its death too alive. It was a volcano.

But it wasn't just <u>like</u> one; there was, in fact, a volcano that had just erupted in Finland, Ida found out later, just like the forecast had predicted. So they were going that way for a reason. The plane was traveling to the U.S. the long way. "But," Ida thought, "The long way to where? Am I ever going to get home?"

Six hours later, she found herself at home, but a home long forgotten.

She decided to take a hotel in the center of Moscow. When she arrived, something was popping up in her mind; something was trying to speak, trying to tell her something; but for a reason she did not know, she wouldn't let herself reveal it to her herself. Ida needed something to take her mind off herself, off her life, off her feeling, off her hopes, off her complaints. Something she could understand and feel as itself.

Ida opened the book; with its pages so white and crisp, soft and fresh, smooth and living: telling the story of life.

Δ Δ Δ

Mr. Bombompsky woke up to the sound of chirping birds: a sound much, much better than a bothersome alarm clock. His mind wandered and he started contemplating juggling.

Juggling was all about balance and timing. Very similar to life, he thought. So much of it is managing time. Balancing. Knowing how to use the limited, constrained time one has when tossing multiple objects in the air. Knowing when to just relax, to think of it as a calm, soothing movement: up, down, catch, throw. Like understanding your priorities, knowing when to do more of what you love, less of what you don't. Knowing what's right, at the right time, for you. You as yourself. Not for parents, not for friends, not for expectations. But for you.

Mr. Bombompsky envisioned the whirling colors of the juggling balls as they whizzed through the air, saying, "Ha ha, you can't catch me!" without actually saying it. Juggling balls had their priorities straight. And then he thought of the fire; he loved when people juggled with rings of fire. When someone does such a daring thing like tossing fire between their hands, they must have pure determination and know they will succeed. They won't burn, because they know they can. They know they can do it. Yes. They can.

And flames. Mr. Bombompsky had always loved those taunting flames, for they brought such boldness and audaciousness and happiness and life. Fire is so alive in all its forms, he thought: in a forest, waiting to have a forest fire; on a campground ready to cook s'mores; on a grill in the back yard grilling hamburgers; in the tiny box of matches labeled "Jet Blue"; in the lighter stuffed in a drawer; on the tip of a candle, a breath waiting to be blown; in the atmosphere creating earth; and in our minds, lighting up with ideas.

Mixes of red, orange, yellow, and then finally smoke. Fire is so alive because it happens, it is becoming and dying all at once, every second of every minute of every hour of everyday, and it is just the bottom line of how things are created, and just, just, happiness and anger mixed together! Fire, as itself and as a representation, is the very being that is us—us yesterday, us today, and us tomorrow.

And imagine fire being thrown into the air, exactly how the Earth turns everyday, mixing and balancing with two other forms of fire, precisely like the mixed emotions and sudden bursts of ideas of all beings, and being caught by a hand, just like we always have a hand, someone, or something, to lean on or to go to or to get comfort from. It matches in all ways. It *is*.

"Oh, gosh, I should be a philosopher!" Mr. Bombompsky thought. That is, I already am one.

Just like he always loved to think of new answers and representations, this was a statement that left an unanswered question—a new conversation. This was exactly what he thought one should do when considered a "genius," because for him, a "genius" to himself, to his fire and light, always gave him something more to think about and was a door to new possibilities.

Ah, Mr. Bombompsky sighed, and then smiled. His smile was happy, so happy, though so calm and relaxed at the same time. Happy as in happy to be alive, happy for today, happy for now.

"Time to write the paragraph that you are going to say at the lecture!" he pseudo-happily told himself. And it was as if another side of him said, "Stop bothering me. I don't want to write that now."

And the two sides kept disputing; kept fighting, and Mr. Bombompsky watched it all. How was he watching himself? He was just another part of himself, just like everyone has many different parts: the happy and delighted part, the slightly upset part, the greedy part, the mad part, the relaxed part. All of those are one—all feelings, those and others, make up a person, make up one. One of the many ones.

How many of us can there be? How many of us are there? Are we all there? Where is there? Is there here? Is here there? Are we here and there? What and who are we? Are we what is here, and there? Are we everywhere? What? What, what? What, what, what?

Mr. Bombompsky took that breath that people make after doing something challenging, or going through a hardship. He inhaled the air and it filled his nostrils, his stomach blew up, his cheeks grew and he made his lips into an "o" and slowly exhaled: exhaled a breath, a precious breath, a loved breath, a human breath, a living breath, a "we" breath. Because he was part of "we," just like every "one" is, and "we" become "us," and "us" become the people. *The* people.

But the people of what?

"I am a people!" he thought. Something about that word, and the way he said it, "peo-ple," made it sound so alive, so bold, and the way he pronounced each and every one of those letters "p-e-o-p-l-e," was so ornate, and the letters seemed so smart and audacious, in a way.

And then Mr. Bombompsky's mind turned away from people and he started to think about his train of thought. Then he thought about the fact that now he was thinking about thinking about thinking, and how all these thoughts had emerged and become real because he was in this very room, with that chirping bird outside still perched on the window sill, with that very cheese sandwich now in his stomach, in that very country, on this very planet called "Earth." All the things he had just discovered only had happened because he was here now, here on Earth, here today. This was home.

Then he snapped back to reality.

Mr. Bombompsky stopped right in mid-air, trying to "snap back to reality". He stopped. He waited.

In books, especially in modern ones, that was a very popular story line, "snapping back to reality." So he had decided to try it out in his "reality."

And Mr. Bombomspky had always had the sense that it would do something, change something: make him feel something different.

But it was just, just, just strange. Because nothing did happen. He didn't "suddenly realize he had been dreaming," because he hadn't, or "had been in an uninteresting meeting and just became aware of his sudden daydream," or "had just been reading and gotten so into the book that he had forgotten where he was." No. Those were all too common scenarios in books.

But no. He had been, in some way, "*snapped* out of his thought." The train (remember the train of thought), had come to its final stop, and its gas was running low, and it was ready to take a break.

Now very pleased with his recent discovery, all in the course of, about, three minutes (it is quite amazing how so many ideas and so much thought can be thought in such little time), Mr. Bombompsky flopped down on his bed, folded his hands like a teacher waiting for his students to do the same, and relaxed.

Right when his dreams were about to overcome him, he had a most brilliant idea. What if there was a Word Market, full of phrases, sentences, paragraphs, and single words? Where you could browse the market, purchase new words every now and then, and expand your vocabulary every day? It would be such a comforting place to have words surround him.

There would be papers and pens, and bags full of ideas, and letters, some even on sale. The C's would be crunchy, though partially cold, and the B's would taste like scrumptious biscuits with little bits of B's butter. The S's would taste like mini, freshly picked strawberries, while the R's would taste like sweet and sour raspberries.

Oh, the feasts in that world would be delicious. What if you could order a letter, just one, single letter, and you would get all the foods in the whole world that begin with it? Take J, for example: Jambalaya, Jicama, Juice, Jackfruit, Jam, Jerk Chicken, Jell-O, and Jellybeans. What a feast.

All the food created a wonderful, imaginary aroma of smells and tastes, but also a cornucopia of colors. He looked out the window to the morning light, and suddenly, it was a symphony of smells and tastes, and magical colors filling the sky.

Even thoughts created such vivid sceneries.

As he thought about all the possibilities of "B" foods, he stumbled upon Baguettes and Bread. The French had the best bread imaginable! The crusts, always perfectly crunchy on top and the soft dough in the inside—and they were always made fresh, so sometimes, he could still feel the heat from the brick ovens in the scrumptious, deliciously delicate dough.

Mr. Bombompsky walked to his suitcase and got out his pale, brown and gold zig-zag tie, a yellow long-sleeve button down shirt, and brown corduroys. The tie looked like a baguette, fresh out of the oven, and then he started giggling like a child. Just enjoying the moment, as some say.

When he finished getting dressed, he took his keys, wallet, and shoes, and walked out the door, whistling an old French tune.

Le muscles célestes,

Le décoverte,

L'Alphabet des revelations.

L'Évidence éternalle!

Grelots roses, ceils en lambeaux:

L'Arbre de la science.

CHAPTER FIFTEEN

The Place of Memory

THE NEXT MORNING, IDA awoke to the bright morning light

gushing out of the window. The trees shook, sprouting leaves of all colors. The usual brown and green leaves were now not crinkly and rumpled but bold fresh, because they were glowing—they really were living.

Ida looked farther out the window and saw all the Russians walking with their carts, driving small automobiles, and riding rusty, old bicycles. Then she looked out the other window and saw an image of New York City; big trucks and limousines, hot dog stands, skyscrapers, huge buildings, benches, parks, stores, and so many advertisements.

What a difference, New York City and Moscow. So different, so far away.

She looked out the window once more. Almost immediately, she got up, threw on black corduroy pants, and a warm, blue crewneck shirt. She put on her grey leather boots and was out of the hotel room in an instant.

Her mind, once again, had two sides: two instincts. Where in the world was she going? What was she doing? But deeper inside her head (full to the brim of emotions she could not control), she knew exactly where and exactly why.

But the ability to phrase thoughts was harder than knowing, and letting go of those thoughts was even harder. Ida's body hurt as she scrambled down the carpeted hotel stairs and stormed out the door. She quickly walked down the sidewalk, turning left, then right, then straight, then left again.

What, why, when, who, where, how?

And she stabbed that question, not wanting to think about it at all, not wanting it to live; because she did know.

But she didn't want to know. Inside, she was about to blow up with "I don't knows," but on the outside she showed a false expression, and... and... why? She rubbed her hands on her face, as if she was hiding herself from herself, not wanting to let go and realize the truth. She rubbed those hands until her face stung, and she kept walking and walking. Suddenly, she came to a sharp halt. And so did the rest of the city: the cars skidded to a stop, the pedestrians' carts hit a bump, the dogs stopped barking, the cats stopped meowing, and the beggars stopped shaking their cups and pleading for change.

Her eyes, mouth, and nose came to an odd position, and her feet were in the middle of taking a step, but then—right then—she saw it. She looked around, unsure of what to do but actually positively knowing what to do. What a battle her two sides were having. She looked around again to see if anyone was watching her, but everyone seemed to be frozen, waiting.

A spotlight seemed to be shining on Ida. This was her moment. But her moment for what?

I am not a pop star starring in a movie, or a Broadway actor, or a famous somebody, or a millionaire. I am just me, Ida. I don't know who I am.

She starred at the wooden door in front of her, with the big brass knocker, when a crumpled piece of paper fell swiftly though gently to the ground. She gasped, then picked it up so quickly, grabbing it like it was her life—and to her, it was her life.

Ida slowly turned the weathered paper around and saw a faded picture of a smiling girl missing two front teeth, grinning so very happily. She looked at the photo and realized it was her, in another dimension, in another world, in another time: as if she had just woken up from a dream and was trying to remember it. But it was hard, almost impossible to remember dreams, or at least the beginning of them.

"But I am not in a dream! This is real! This is me; still is me! I am this, this is me, me, me, me! It is reality, and my thinking that it is a dream is also reality, so why can't I just accept it?"

Once again, Ida felt that tug inside of her, that pull of emotions, a string being untied. Once again she heard the music, her theme song. A fiddler, playing a tune, a young boy strumming an acoustic guitar, a young couple, and the young girl, her fingers moving like a fish running from a shark and creating a world of sound.

Ida shoved away that thought but others poured in. A boy in a grey coat and black pants with ripped holes on the knee with a blue cap... a woman with her hair in a bun kissing a child goodnight... a boy and girl on a swing in front of a school next to a construction site... the boy coming closer to her lips... the slamming of doors... whispers of voices... and flying piano notes.

"No! No, no, no!"

Ida screamed between sudden gulps of air. She reached out, trying to grasp something, trying to hang on, trying to live the moment, trying to think but not to feel...

And the thoughts in her mind became more real, more vivid, more alive. She was flying through water, through fire, through the crack of time, through her own mind, traveling somewhere, deep into her own projections and memories.

The fire seemed to burn her flesh, but the water seemed to cool it, one doing something, the other the opposite.

"What is going on?" She asked herself.

She knew. But all she knew was that she knew. That was the only knowing she had.

She walked faster, picking up her pace. She didn't know where she was going, but her heart knew. Her mind knew.

As Ida turned the corner, she stopped suddenly. She slowly looked up, and the sign came to full view. This was the concert hall, the one with real velvet plush seats and red carpets, where she had performed her first piano concert.

Ida remembered that day so clearly: that gorgeous, luscious, fabulous day on which her life truly started.

Then she understood. Music had saved her. Music was her true family, and it would never die. It would never judge, only be a friend. Music was her lifelong companion.

But then her hand, without any commands from her brain, reached into the pocket book and pulled out a small book, a book with a brown, leather cover, and opened it to the 59th page, and started grasping sentences, throwing them down her throat, trying to avoid her own mind and storming into someone else's so she wouldn't have to feel it, feel her own feelings. She wanted to leave them alone, to leave them, to not torture herself, but it was all too complicated.

She had to. Her fingers slowly turned the page, forcing her to read the words because she knew she wanted to escape, and suddenly—

It was as if her mind had gone blank, empty, done, collapsing and leaving her with only one option. One crack. One truth. One story. One life.

Deeper down the crack: The book. Her projection. Her models. Her real family. They were taking over.

Δ Δ Δ

Mr. Bombompsky had just finished the book meeting. As he wandered out of the wooden door of the cobblestone cottage that served as the bookstore, he was half daydreaming. How he loved to hear people speak and say truly smart, interesting things.

As he strolled along the pavement he passed a few different stores, occasionally stepping in and saying hello to the shopkeepers, and just walking around for the pleasure of walking, until he came to Café Regular. Only then he decided he should quench his thirst.

As he stepped in, he steered himself in the direction of the counter, where he eyed a delicious looking chocolate chip scone and an Orangina. He got in line, and when it was his turn, said a quick, friendly hello to the barman, ordered, and paid—exactly 3.27£.

He walked to an empty table, wiped off the crumbs, and sat down. Mr. Bombompsky twisted off the blue cap of his drink, and the bubbly fizz poured out. He brought the bottle to his lips and smiled at the sweet, orangey taste.

Mr. Bombompsky loved illustrations. They were another way to tell stories. And that's why the three cards, face up, with colorful pictures on them laying on the table next to him caught his eye.

He leaned over, trying to catch a better glimpse of the cards. His eyes were stunned at the color and the ornate drawings. The pictures were depicting a bigger story. Maybe they were story cards, or even—

"Excuse me," said a voice, with an obvious hint of a Spanish accent. "Excuse me, but you're about to fall off your chair!"

Mr. Bombompsky shot right up, his eyes focused on the man.

"Thank you," he mumbled. "I, I, was just try-trying to get a better luh-luh...look at those cards you have. They're quite beautiful."

The man smiled a mischievous smile, then quickly rearranged it to be more serious. "What cards?" he said slowly.

"Why, *those* cards of course," Mr. Bombompsky turned to face the table, and pointed to exactly where the cards had been, then looked up, puzzled.

He thought for a moment, then said, "Where did you put them?" But he said this in a very calm and serious voice.

"I can see you have an eye! So you must have a mind too, eh?"

Mr. Bombompsky looked puzzled, but slowly started to understand.

"Come," the man said.

And Mr. Bombompsky's first instinct was to do just that.

"Welcome to the world of Tarot."

CHAPTER SIXTEEN

I Am the Book

IDA STEPPED OUT OF the plane. She was now in Sweden and in two hours would board another plane to Montreal, Canada and then yet another to New York City.

The expression on her face wasn't sad nor gloomy, but it wasn't happy either. It was a face that described living—or at least the living of Ida. Her shoulders were slightly hunched, but her neck was straight, and her short, boy-length hair, combed, sat nicely on top of her head like it did every day.

She wasn't going to get coffee this time.

Not in the mood for a snack or drink, Ida walked towards a bookstore, called "Sagor av Living Besvärad", "Tales of the Living Mind". The name seemed to overpower her brain, appealing to her. So she walked in.

As she strolled around, Ida spotted a soft, black cover book labeled "IDA". Immediately, though slowly, she turned to the back cover:

This is the story of Ida, whose life consists mainly of resting, because she is always tired: tired of talking to herself; and of music—high notes and low.

The New York Times raves: "One might call it a short novel, or a long poem, or a scale, going left to right, from low, deep notes, to light happy ones, on a grand, gold Steinway piano. A beautiful masterpiece."

Ida flipped to the first page. But first, without reading it, she turned through the pages as if it were a flipbook. On every page where the page number should have been, it was labeled:

I **D** *A*

On the first page, the IDA labeling was ten times bigger: it covered the whole page.

Ida was born in Moscow in the Balnitsa Hospital, close to the center square.

No, I wasn't. It was on the outskirts of town.

She was born to two gentle and loving parents.

My mother hardly cared about me.

Ida lived in a huge house, and she was one of three children. Her room was in the middle of the top floor.

My house was an average size, and my youngest brother, Victor died when he was two. My room was in the attic, and I used to share it with him

Her youngest brother, Vector, was the odd exception of the three. He wailed every night, while the other children went to bed obediently.

My brother cried because he was smart. He made attempts to get out because he hated being cooped up. And his name was Victor, not Vector!

Ida didn't fully respect her brother. She didn't like his name.

I loved him so much. And I didn't even pay attention to the name.

At eight years old, she met a boy whom she adored tremendously. They became best friends and had fabulous times laughing and playing together. But when they both turned nine, a tragedy struck. Ida's mother was in an accident. Ida wasn't truly upset. She wasn't very fond of her mother, but did, however, feel slightly bad. It was a terrible combination of emotions.

The father, alone with the three children, had to sell the house and the family moved away. But the boy loved her, though there was nothing he could do. He never gave up.

The two children had the same birthday, and on his tenth birthday, the boy, lost hope. He stuck the photo, his favorite one of the two of them, in the door of her old house. It showed him and Ida laughing. But it was ripped in half, and he kept the half of himself.

Secretly, the boy hoped for the rest of his life that Ida would come back, see the photo, and remember.

Why do you have to be so wrong, though so right? Ida thought. Gentle tears spilled out of her watery eyes. She didn't want to be crying right then and there. It was not the moment to let it all out.

And yet the tears kept rolling out, smothering her soft, rosy cheeks, a river finally flowing through the mountains after a long, hot, dry summer.

She wanted to pretend she was cutting an onion so she could have something to blame for making her cry.

CHAPTER SEVENTEEN

Reading and Being: the Tarot

As HE CLIMBED THE hill, Mr. Bombompsky could see the vast

blue-green water of the Mediterranean Sea. He thought about all the sparks of life and civilization that had occurred here through time. Now he would be part of the chain, part of that story.

The bookstore wasn't too far off in the distance; he could already see the purple awning with its gold lettering. As he read the ornate writing on it, he knew it was the correct place.

He was walking in France, in Marseille, down a cobblestone road near the Coeur de Julien. He walked through the door of a bookstore, and finally sat in the blue chair smack in the middle of the cream-colored room. All the while, he was holding his cream puff with its soft dough on the outside and puffy cream bursting out from the top, coated in chocolate syrup.

It was a fairly big crowd that surrounded him; it looked like over fifty people. There was a bar for drinks on the edge that had a butcher-block counter and various tables for customers. The walls, however, were completely covered with books.

The books were old—cracks could be seen in the many colored spines. But he could tell: something about the books told him that they were not the typical old books covered with rips and dust; these books were not just old, they had lived a long time and were very, very knowledgeable.

This was not just a bookstore, but a lovingly and carefully curated collection of authors' works, including limited editions, interviews, special printings, personal letters and correspondences, even first manuscripts written by hand. Whoever sorted out this library and put it together must have had a true love of literature.

Mr. Bombompsky felt some sort of connection.

He noticed the plump French women sitting in the corner serving snacks: slices of Croque Monsieur. She had short, curly, bright black hair, bright red lipstick, and bright blue almond shaped eyes. Next to her was a very tall, slim woman who also seemed to be French. He looked at her, then at the other woman.

He studied the other woman, then looked back at her.

He carefully examined her, and then turned his gaze back to the other woman.

He shook his head.

The whole place filled him with a unique feeling, like he was in a community of real literature, of real writing and story telling and imagination and experiences. It was truly his world.

Suddenly, his eyes caught sight of the cards, and he realized that the lecture had begun.

"Welcome, everybody," said the man in the black suit. "We are gathered here today to explore the deep, rich world of the tarot. As you may know, art is always an event of becoming, an encounter, a way to be present to one's self. And today, my friends, you will soon learn that so is the tarot."

The crowd seemed to cheer through their eyes. Everyone was studying the man. There was a very quiet silence in the room. But it was, like silence mostly is, a wave, occasional whispers surfacing from various spots around the room.

"Let me tell something about these cards that you see in front of you. These cards, they open the field to countless projections, and a thousand meanings can be attributed to each one, each of which can be right at a given moment. It is the time when we have to stop imagining what would please us, what we want the fortune to say or express, and to start accepting, and feeling. You must remember: the interpretations are inexhaustible."

He took a pause before choosing nine cards from the deck. He lay them out in a three by three array on top of a cloth-covered round table next to him. He flipped over one of the cards and began once again.

"The major tone of this card concerns pleasure and emotional life. It depicts just that, and the rest you alone must relate to your own life. There is always a relation to be made, even if it is not quite clear.

REYNE DE BASTON·

"Now you may think that this card is very simple; it plainly shows a lady in robes whose eyes point towards the floor. But it may not be that simple. Today, simplicity is a common response to problems, to fears, to disagreements—you've heard the expression 'take the easy way out,' no? Easy, simple. But it's not as simple as that. Because to make something appear simple, it takes a lot of hard work. One must be able to truly understand the underlying challenges before he can come up with an elegant solution. And that involves digging through the depths of complexity. There are so many ways to go with everything, but only part of it can be seen by the eye. And that is why we have to dig deeper."

The words began to swim and wash over Bombompsky, and he let them flow to an inner space inside himself. Nevertheless, Jodorowsky's calming voice continued.

"But all of the cards point to the same question: is the body in the spirit, or the spirit in the body? And that may not even be the right question; is there more to life than one's "fate?" An afterlife? A second being within you even though you cannot see it?

The tarot is a way, one way, that starts to define. But it is only a beginning, my friends.

"It is a fundamental principle that tarot readers must have; and that is to be able to go past what the card looks like, to go past our sudden instinct; and to most of all, have the strength to do it."

Mr. Bombompsky thought of how often he would not allow himself to see the thing that was right in front of him, to really see the moment.

Things were as they appeared, but it was only a matter of letting yourself see them. So many times, he had been frightened and not able, closing his eyes, blocking them from what was really there. Sometimes situations can be so scary that we force ourselves to turn away because we feel that is the only sense of protection. But Jodorowsky was right: we can not turn away from the world as it is but, we need to have the strength to see it. As he continued, a reassuring strength came upon Bombompsky—the kind of fearlessness that he had imagined for Lee Cot would now be his own. He began to imagine that the characters of his novel were like his own set of tarot cards, each expressing his strengths, fears, imaginings and desires, and that as a writer, his novel was a vehicle for his expression and exploration for his luxurious appetites and psyche. It was a cartography, a map for him to interpret and understand himself.

"All of you here, you must have come here for a reason. Just think about it. Maybe your friend recommended coming, or your wife insisted, or you just wanted to come. But when you really do think about it, there is much more 'reasoning' behind that reason of why you came: a whole story to that simple matter.

"I had at the age of seven my first contact with the cards. According to my friend's philosophy, at the age of seven, a child's brain is already formed and should be treated as an adult. I asked myself, 'What do these cards do?' And I realized that wasn't the right question to begin with; rather, 'What did they mean?' And it was then that I started to explore meanings, definitions, and interpretations. And the tarot was with me that whole time."

He paused, taking in a deep breath. One person in the crowd slowly lifted up their hand.

"Yes?"

"You know, it has always been a question to me; how do people stand what they do, emotionally and physically, if it truly intertwines with their mind and can affect your feeling? How do you do it? Stand it? I mean, you must have tried to understand each one of those cards, and you must have tried to tell your own fate, your reason and meaning in life. But what triggers your brain to keep with it, to stay with it and never give up, to truly be determined to keep living with the continuous possibilities that may come up with these simple cards?"

"The tarot is a world in itself. It appears as a deck of cards, with images on one side of the card. It can be interpreted in two ways: the literal appearance, or what you make of it. Life is all about interpretations— there are thousands of interpretations to be made about each and every single thing on this earth. And I do it by truly feeling my emotions. Life is full of feelings. Anger, sadness, suffering. And joy. But when you take the lessons of the suffering, of truly feeling your emotional self, you start to realize that you are not the center of the world. You are one center, but not the center. Every one of us is a center of the universe.

But the mistake is to think, "I am the only center." And not the persons around me. You need to learn you have value. Not to be a person who says, "I am not the center, I am nothing. Nothing at all." You need to diminish on one side, and on the other side you need to grow. That is the Work. You need to be able to balance, in the middle, of accepting and truly adoring yourself, while at the same time understanding others, ideas, and different ways. And the tarot just describes; it leads to what you may think of as understanding.

"In every self—myself, yourself—we have eternal sunshine, eternal darkness, eternal madness, eternal hatred, and eternal liveliness. We all wish to be eternal, but the question is: which way will we choose to be it?"

Everyone looked at Jodorowsky in deep silence, and they all tried to grasp this talkative man's intriguing statements. Of all the 63 people in the room, each one was thinking something different.

"Underneath each picture on each card, there is a whole story to be told. But you must know: there is no prize to be had once you know your story. It isn't about a reward. It may regale you, or bring a cape of darkness to your soul. But truly, the most important is to not have expectations. This is something where you truly need to block out any cacophony and sound of any sort. You need to push out all the whispers and voices that lodge in your head; just listen and look."

Jodorowsky's eyes met Bombompsky's, and because of it, a moment later Bompompsky was sitting next to him in the center of the circle, and in front of his gaze lay three cards, face down.

Bombompsky felt unusually calm, maybe even joyous; something deeper than mere happiness—the kind of happiness that does not depend on what happens. And there he saw it. He was perfectly receptive to the moment, right in the moment, without time.

The hand swiftly turned over the card, and it seemed as if time had stretched, and one second lasted a minute. It was the slow motion of life. Then the card had been opened, ready to tell a story.

LE·BATELEUR

"Oh. I see it now," said Jodorowsky, a thoughtful smile emerging onto his face.

"What?" Mr. Bombompsky nervously asked.

"What do you think?"

He interpreted the first card, and then the second, perfectly content and happy with his mild but deep and interesting life. No disappointment.

Then came the third. It looked like this:

Mr. Bombompsky looked puzzled. He turned to Jodorowsky, who looked as if he were holding back something so strong, so real, and so not good.

Δ Δ Δ

Mr. Bombompsky considered those words on his third day back home, taking a walk along the streets of his neighborhood. His mind was still so angry, so confused, so bewildered. What had that last tarot card meant?

When one doesn't know the answer, he usually assumes the worst. And that was exactly what Mr. Bombompsky had gotten himself into.

He didn't know what to think anymore. It was as if his brain had been knocked over, kicked with all the strength in the world. He had worked so hard to try to understand himself, and he did that through writing. He loved the sense of authorship, to have created beautiful sentences.

But all that was over. His fate had been told, and fate can't be changed.

As he walked down President street, he noticed a small garden planted around a tree trunk, along with flowers and other plants. His eye cornered a lush, purple, perfectly ripe eggplant.

Oh, how that eggplant wanted him, and he wanted it. He knew the eggplant was meant for him: its beauty was undeniable.

And at that moment, he understood. Writing had brought him closer to himself, to his mind, his energy to his being. Each of his characters was a facet of himself. He loved Lee Cot. Lee Cot was that soaring, invincible, phantom that could conquer it all if he wanted. To be able to create someone that could do that made Mr. Bombompsky feel so good about himself. Emil was the younger version of Mr. B—the youth that he still had.

He couldn't abandon it. How could someone ever leave something that had provoked and changed their life? Writing was a gift, one that would never be returned.

Now, it was time to cook himself, to create himself, to taste his passion, personality, and love once again. Mr. Bombompsky threw away the memory of the tarot and decided that fortune, fate, or whatever you call it could never be told, but only lived. And one could only live that for oneself.

He picked up the eggplant and held it tightly, as if it were a newborn baby. He smelled the luxurious smell of freshness, and took in the aroma of what he knew as life

CHAPTER EIGHTEEN

The End Ends It All

LATER THAT EVENING, MR. Bombompsky sat in his living room on his comfy couch. With a fresh, determined mind, he set out to finish the story of Lee Cot.

Δ Δ Δ

In less than 15 minutes, however, when the sand storm dissipated, and all the rage and noise and cacophony of Sir E. Vil exhausted itself, the waterfall of sand stopped. Lee Cot saw with no blur at all, in clear sight, the giant question mark, like a rainbow after a storm.

Now, he would simply take it to the top of the mountain.

His days in the desert had taught him that there were energies and feelings that could not be ordinarily described with the instruments of everyday life. In a way, he was saddened that there was no way to explain this to others—like poetry, or music. Unless you hear it or see it or feel it, you wouldn't know it.

It enlightened him too. He had come to understand, he had come to dig a deeper level of the maze of life.

The question mark had appeared at the right moment. It was manifest, just like all his energies had come to him from some deep, unknown place in time. It was right. It felt right.

Later, Lee Cot and his horse found themselves zipping up the mountain, navigating their way, every millisecond getting closer to the jackpot, dragging the question mark behind them. Oh, this was such a wondrous moment!

His time was probably a time that would not be recorded in history, though. Stories like Lee's just never got told. It was always the iPods, the iPhones, the electronics, the models, the actors that got remembered in the future.

But why wasn't it about people like Lee Cot, who really were the ones who spent life trying to define it?

But never mind that. Lee Cot was doing this for his people and himself, no matter his legacy. Right?

Life is a balance: a scale with one side holding the utopian qualities of life, the other the dystopian. And that in itself is perfect.

If one is happy their whole life, how will they know what happiness really feels like, if they have no change, no variations, no experimentations? But when things go wrong, and then when you are happy, you know you're not feeling bad so the happiness becomes a true feeling.

See, people are happy for many reasons. But joy comes mostly from overpowering dissatisfaction, from overcoming fear and, say, "unhappiness."

And at that moment, that very moment when Lee Cot couldn't breathe, when his lungs were screaming, when his whole body was burning, when he was hauling the big, big question mark to the top of the hill, when he looked down to see Sir E. Vil struggling just a few feet below him, when he saw the mountaintop so near, so close, when he was about to grasp the future in his hands. Lee Cot felt that unhappiness flow out of him, his anger, pain, and struggle floated away, and then, right then, as the dot of the question mark touched the very top of the hill, he felt the happiness, the thrill, the excitement flood, pound into his body.

He had done it.

He stood up, off his horse, proudly holding the question mark on the hill.

He had done it.

He placed the question mark onto the base where it would stand for the next ten years, determining a future of new possibilities, of new questions.

He had done it.

And there he stood, cheering for himself, for his effort, for his dystopian-utopia-of-a-life. That was good enough for him.

Δ Δ Δ

Mr. Bombompsky smiled to himself. But it was more then just a smile. It was a smile of completion.

Δ Δ Δ

Ida sat at the piano back home in her cozy apartment, all the things she loved surrounding her. The sun shone in through the glass window, and outside the autumn leaves fell slowly to the ground. Her fingers slowly crawled to the piano, and music steadily filled the room. It was gingery, it had a tinge of sweet, some sour, but somehow it was gingery; that was the word.

She changed from a light scale to a deep, figurative melody rich with the pedal. Ida moved her head swiftly from side to side, elaborately moving her fingers across the piano.

The music created a deep, emotional though extravagant mood throughout the room, and it was so alive. Ida could almost feel the music—it was within her, it was she, and she was it.

Δ Δ Δ

Eating bites of his home cooked meal, saving the eggplant for last, Mr. Bombompsky sat at his kitchen table with a pad and pen.

Δ Δ Δ

Ah. I stretched my arms out along the side of my bed, waking up for real now. All my consciousness was bonding together and letting me wake up; all my senses were able to work.

I sat up, and rolled my shoulders round and round. They felt so strong, so new, so alive. My cough had disappeared, my runny nose was gone, and I was steadily regaining my strength. I looked outside, and the sun was blaring from its spot in the sky.

I thought for that moment of the heavy, heavy steps of my grandma coming up the stairs. I thought about the weight of the body, and the weight of emotions, and then the weight of social bonds of people and their families, and the social organization of life, of community and friendship.

My mind soared around through thoughts, philosophy, and meaning. I thought for a while.

I guess I was really trying to understand. To figure out something that I wasn't yet ready to define.

But mostly, I felt so good. I had finished Lee Cot's story! Maybe, just maybe, I would write a second one! For the moment, though, I felt brilliant.

A little while later, I heard someone coming up the stairs. The sound in my ears must have cleared, because the thunderous stomping of my Grandma seemed to have disappeared. I now heard light, gentle footsteps walking up the stairs.

And as the door to my room opened, I was sure my grandmother had changed. She walked to my bed, and noticing that I was better, she started the whole ritual of "I'm so glad you're feeling better, sweetheart."

About an hour later, I found myself sitting on a beach blanket on the grassy meadow of the local park. As I bit in to my prosciutto and swiss cheese sandwich on rye, I started to imagine Lee Cot, and how he was a mystic cowboy, how he could do anything at anytime he wanted, and how he really could leave his body and move into different dimensions of time. Lee Cot really was my desire to exceed the body, to go beyond it and through it—he was my space-time continuum. Yeah!

While I thought about this, my mouth was full of pure deliciousness and yumminess as I took the most mouth-watering bite of my classic rye bread sandwich. It is a simple fact of life that while extravagance is always preferred, simple things can be just as rich, just like my meat and cheese sandwich.

I was tasting that very bite in my mouth, that only my tongue could taste, and yet my mind, which is in this (my) very body, was contemplating about my fictional masterpiece known as my character, and yet my mouth was urging to take another bite. And what struck me was that all of this was happening at once. Was I in two places right then because that was happening all in unison? Or is it all one? Can I actually affect a faraway space with my thought? Or can only Lee Cot, my very own telekinetic cowboy, do that?

And there it was, during that bite, between the bread in my mouth and the thoughts in my mind, between this reflection of Lee Cot and all the dialectics of life in his character. He toiled with my mind to go beyond everyday thinking, to go beyond average, to go beyond these distinctions, to imagine and believe and create. Were cherry pies and cherries really that different? Or was it just a cherry going to a more complex level of excitement? Or the idea, the language through words, that a red ball of juicy fruit was called a cherry? Lee Cot (even though I had yet to write about him) was my very mind in different shoes; an eager detective ready to accomplish anything.

And so I thought about how our society today has created so many opposites; black and white, big and small, soft and hard, high and low. Rationality and intuition were all false dichotomies. There was no body separate from spirit. It was just body-spirit. All that had been separated out for us to understand, all this separation was false. It is what you make of it, not of what the average, everyday person thinks, because there is no average, everyday person, because every average, everyday person is one's own self, and no two selfs are the same. And Lee Cot would be my fictional construction that allowed me to go beyond rational thinking, to be both in the body and in the waves of time itself.

And the treasure that he would find would be the true understanding of this.

The one thing I knew for sure was that having relationships, even with something or someone that is not exactly real, is extraordinary. The bond between Lee Cot, a character who didn't quite know me as well as I knew him, and I, proved just that. And just the fact that I call us, Lee Cot and I, "we" proves that anything can be connected to anything.

Life has no limits or breakpoints or finish lines. Life is only the new step to continuing: to keep going.

I looked up to the sky to see a kite in the shape of a bird soaring about. The kite glided with the wind; a bond within itself. I traced my eyes down the string that kept the kite from floating away, and surprisingly, it was my grandmother who was steering the bird. She was looking at the kite with a gaze of satisfaction, of affection.

I stood up, took one last bite of my sandwich, and ran to join her. I put my arm around hers, and she hugged me back.

Together we watched the kite fly through the sky, dodging the clouds, and creating a soothing rhythm as it flew in small circles throughout the air.

As my thoughts rejoined me after minutes of focusing on the sky, I thought about stories. If Lee Cot was real, or at least real within his story, wouldn't he be wondering who was creating him; who was writing him? Wouldn't he be curious to understand his author?

And then, I started considering this crazy thought that I might not even be real in reality, and that someone might be writing me.

Δ Δ Δ

Mr. Bombompsky sat up in delight.

And then he started wondering himself: what if I am a character in a book?

Δ Δ Δ

Ida looked up from her book and smiled. What a beautiful ending.

And then she thought: what if I myself am in a story right now too? What if someone is reading me at this very moment?

Δ Δ Δ

"And that, children, is the end of this novel." The man looked up from his leather chair, and smiled at the classroom of children in front of him.

ACKNOWLEDGEMENTS

I'D LIKE TO ACKNOWLEDGE the people who truly helped me throughout the process of writing my work of fiction. My friend and often employer Maragret Heatherman. Thank you for your multiple readings and edits and generosity of time. Thank you to Kate Hosford, Laura Tisdale, Ben Greenman, Melanie Oser, Daniel Coffeen, Mr. Paulmer, Sina Zekavat, and Hannah Lola Verhulst. for your inputs and encouragement. To my parents, for really making sure I brought my story into the world: Marc Lafia, my father, who was an incredible spark to the utter creativity of this book; to Irena, my mom, who really edited my entire book and helped me the whole way. To all the members of my book club, who chose my very own novel as the monthly book and showered me with fantastic enthusiasm. Thank you to the universe, especially through my travels, for inspiring my writing then, now, and forever.

ABOUT THE AUTHOR

LOLA LAFIA WROTE THIS book while traveling through Europe during the summer of 2011. She loves the relationship of fantasy and realism, books and stories, fiction and reality—and incorporated it all in her debut novel, The Crack. The story was inspired through observations during her travels, endless conversations with her father, interests and curiosities, and spur of the moment ideas. Over the next year, she kept working, editing, and revisiting her work until she found the perfect balance of great literature and correct grammar. Lola lives in Park Slope, Brooklyn, and continues to explore, play soccer, design, create, laugh, and write more every day.

Made in the USA
San Bernardino, CA
23 December 2013